MAGIC, MIMOSAS & MISTLETOE

A Charmed Cocktail Cozy

M. L. BONATCH

Cover Art by Spellbinding Designs

Editor: Three Point Author Services

Proofreader: Y.K. Bonatch

FOLLOW ME EVERYWHERE

Follow me to keep up with all my magical mayhem.

- amazon.com/-/e/B0951C41XM
- bookbub.com/authors/m-l-bonatch
- facebook.com/MLBonatch
- twitter.com/mbonatch
- instagram.com/mlbonatch.author
- pinterest.com/maureenbonatch

ABOUT THIS BOOK

I don't see dead people, but my dog does.

Hi, I'm Marissa Hale. When my friend, Grace invites me to visit the Inn she inherited, I'm high-tailing it back to my home state of Pennsylvania. Like most things in life, there are strings attached to her inheritance—and these ones have twinkly lights. The Inn, and the town, are Christmas themed. No witch worth her broom would choose Christmas over Halloween, unless that witch's bloodline is the magic mainline for keeping the yuletide spirit alive.

The death of Grace's aunt was already suspicious, but then we stumble upon a dead body amongst the poinsettias that resembles one of Santa's fabled elves. It sure seems like someone is trying to force Grace to sell Kringle Inn. I'm going to need all the help I can get to solve these crimes, and save Christmas, but when the only witnesses are a pig, and a ghost, I'm not sure that's going to be enough...

MAGIC, MIMOSAS & MISTLETOE

I

"When you said the inn was in Tinsel Village, Pennsylvania, I pictured nightclubs, not Santa's workshop." There were a few key details my friend Grace had neglected to mention. After driving through the night and arriving before dawn, the scene before me made me wonder if I'd fallen asleep and was dreaming. "Inheriting this inn from your Aunt Mid seems to have strings attached—twinkly ones. It looks like the North Pole vomited."

We stood in the foyer, wiping our feet on the Happy Holidays doormat. Mulder, my Shih Tzu, stopped short, his bulbous eyes fixed on an old plastic Santa. The decorations outside had just been an appetizer for the buffet of holiday-everything inside.

"Just what kind of witch was your Aunt Mid? No

witch worth her broom would choose Christmas over Halloween." I stumbled when my dog shot past me, pegging the back of my legs and almost knocking me down with his barrel-like body.

Grace smiled weakly. "I'm sorry, Marissa. I know how you feel about Christmas. If I'd told you the Kringle Inn, and the whole surrounding town, had a year-long holiday theme, you might've changed your mind about coming."

"Christmas? But it's barely Halloween."

Grace flicked the light switch while peering at the ceiling. The remaining functioning lights cast a dim glow over the small lobby. "I used to love the inn as a child." She shrugged. "The place isn't so bad. It just needs a little work."

I hung my coat on the rack. "Are you planning on selling it?" At least *then* the Christmas theme would make sense. Mortals were much more enamored with that holiday year-round.

"Aunt Mid had listed it for a short while before she died. But now that it's mine, I haven't decided." Grace glanced out the window at *the For Sale* sign leaning against the porch. "The realtor must not have picked up the sign yet."

"From the looks of it, she'd have been better off investing more time in the upkeep and less time decorating," I said. The inn looked like it had been around since the beginning of time— tired and wilted like a discarded Christmas tree with a few lingering pieces of tinsel at the end of January.

"My love of the holiday season began with this inn," Grace said with a sigh.

I patted her arm. She was the type of person who decorated trees in every room and started shopping in July.

I glanced around. "Is anyone else here?" My voice echoed from the vaulted ceiling and second floor balcony. The string of lights wrapped throughout the wrought iron balcony railing flickered.

Grace nodded, sending a few red coils of her hair bobbing. "A few staff members stayed on to maintain the upkeep. They should arrive soon."

Mulder's yipping drew my attention. He rarely barked, instead using a multitude of odd sounds as his preferred method of communication. It wasn't often he engaged in a barking rant unless a squirrel or bird taunted him.

"He must've found more decorations to harass." I located his pom-pom-like tail poking out among a bunch of poinsettias.

Jasper slunk over to investigate. Despite his disdain for his furry sibling, the cat couldn't contain his curiosity, and Mulder always found things of interest to the animal species.

"Jasper, stay out of those poinsettias! They're poisonous," I yelled, as if the feline was hard of hearing. The knot in my stomach confirmed I loved the little bugger. Grace was accustomed to my banter with the cat, despite only hearing a bunch of meowing when Jasper spoke to me. She'd accepted it when I told her Jasper and I could communicate after a spell backfired—at least that was what I *thought* had happened.

Jasper got close enough to see what had secured Mulder's attention and turned to respond. "For goddess' sake, woman, it's not like I'm going to eat a plant. I wouldn't stoop to that level. Besides, there's something over here. It smells bad and might be dead."

"What?" Had I heard him correctly over Mulder's barking? "Mulder, that's enough."

I shook my head when the dog regarded me with big pleading eyes. Trying to silence him was a waste of my breath. He ignored the few requests he understood, unless they benefitted him.

"Jasper, did you say dead? You mean a flower, right?" I paused at the edge of the poinsettias and peered over the leaves. "There's practically a forest of these plants."

My foot smacked against something hard and unyielding. As I hopped on one foot to cradle the injured toe of the other, I lost my balance and fell face-forward with a yelp into the flowery forest.

Mulder backed away, whining now that I'd heeded his alert to investigate.

"Marissa, are you alright?" Grace rushed across the tile.

"I think so," I muttered to the floor. My pool of hair occluded my view. I pushed the pink strands away—which clashed with the red flowers—and turned my head. "But I don't think he is."

I pushed to my haunches to keep from falling on my behind while putting distance between me and the corpse. Sadly, this wasn't the first time I'd encountered a dead body. Bad luck seemed to follow me.

"Oh, my goddess," Grace gasped and put a trembling hand over her mouth. The smattering of freckles on her face stood out against her pale skin, giving her the appearance of a specter. "Who is that? And what is he doing there?"

"He's not doing a lot of anything now." I took a deep breath to slow my racing heart and keep my wits about me. "He hasn't been here long."

I pointed to the dried blood surrounding him and staining tile underneath. With a shaky hand, I confirmed he didn't have a pulse and wasn't breathing. If he was a vampire, that wouldn't have made a difference, but he didn't resemble one. "Do you recognize him as one of the staff?"

"No. I wouldn't, though. It's been years since I've been here." Grace pressed a hand to her chest. "Oh, my. This is terrible."

I bent closer to the body. "Is it just me, or does he look like an elf?"

Grace leaned in to peer at the little man wearing green stockings, a pointed cap, and a wide belt cinching his jacket. "It could be a costume," she said.

"Do you see his ears?"

"Okay, it might not be a costume, but we're witches. We are used to the unusual in the world, but this..." Grace crossed her arms, holding herself.

"What did you say your Aunt Mid died from?"

"I assumed it was a natural death. I didn't think to question it. Her health had been failing for years." She turned to me while avoiding looking at the poinsettias. "Why in the world would I think otherwise? Aunt Mid was a sweet old lady. I can't think of a single person who'd want to harm her."

"Okay. You might be right. But don't two deaths at the inn over the past two months appear unusual?"

"Any more unusual than how you talk to your cat?"

She had me there. But Jasper had proven invaluable in helping me solve other crimes. He came in handy as a furry side kick. Mulder helped, too, but more by distracting people with his silly adorableness. Although, this time Mulder *did* find the body.

I must've said the last part aloud because Jasper hissed and suddenly appeared to be ticked off.

"I would've come across it in no time," Jasper said, stalking away.

I stood and peered around the lobby, my gaze focusing on the dark hallway. "A better question is whether the killer is still here."

Grace sighed. "*If* there was a killer. It appears like he fell and hit his head." She pointed with a shaky hand to the Christmas lights tangled around his ankle and then turned away from the body.

"Maybe," I said. But I wasn't convinced. "Why don't you sit down, Grace?" I led her to the couch. The hallway remained in our view from this angle.

Jasper bumped against my legs. "Don't you think you'd better call the police?"

Jasper wasn't usually the voice of reason in our relationship, which made his sensible observation even more disturbing. It showed how unnerved I was. This trip was supposed to be a fun getaway, but it sure wasn't starting out like one.

The cat pawed at me to get my attention. "I'm cold, tired, and I'm starving. We've been driving all night, and it's way past my breakfast time."

"Jasper is right," I said, causing the cat to perk up when I agreed with him. "Not about your breakfast; we'll get to that. But we *do* need to call the police."

A loud *thump* made us all jump and turn toward the top of the stairs.

I squeezed my eyes shut and opened them again, checking to ensure I wasn't seeing things due to lack of sleep. A reindeer might not have surprised me, but *this?*

"Is ... is that a pig?"

Grace didn't respond. She was too busy gaping. The pig's oblong body and hooves would've made descending the sweeping staircase a strategic challenge, but he seemed determined. He lifted his snout and snorted a few times, nostrils twitching, and then studied the stairs.

"What is this?" Jasper arched his back and hissed. "A pig? What is he doing inside? I won't have it! There's no way there will be enough food for everyone if a pig lives here."

I didn't point out how Jasper was making a lot of assumptions. The pig made its way down the stairs, keeping his eyes fixed on Jasper, perhaps sensing that his presence didn't thrill the cat.

"I don't think you have much of a choice," I said. "Besides, he might be a witness. Go see if he'll talk to you."

"Talk to *me*?" Jasper's voice rose to a squeak. "Are you insane?"

I shrugged. "Now, come on, the pig might've seen something that can help us quickly resolve if this wasn't an accidental death." Any death on the property couldn't be good, but confirming it had been an accident would be a start.

Grace may not admit it, but I knew her heart was set on reviving the inn. I wanted to help to make her dream a reality.

Mulder glanced toward the poinsettias and let out an occasional huff, which I could assume was to remind us there were more pressing matters than the pig. Being able to converse with an animal like I could with Jasper sure made things easier.

Jasper stared and hissed at the pig while we phoned the local police station.

The pig, meanwhile, stood at the bottom of the stairs and studied the cat with disinterest.

We'd just settled onto the couch to wait when the sound of a car approaching interrupted the silence. Grace pulled the drapes open, and the rising sun illuminated the lobby—as well as the cobwebs on the stone fireplace mantle.

"That must be Arthur. He's been the caretaker here for as long as I can remember." She opened the door for the old man and rested a hand on his shoulder. "Arthur, it's been too long."

Grace explained to him what she thought had happened—that the victim must've fallen and hit his head, the resulting injury leading to his death—and that we were waiting for the police.

I kept my suspicions to myself about automatically ruling out foul play, especially since Grace didn't believe that anything more than an accident had occurred. But I tended to lean on the side of caution.

Arthur squinted behind his thick glasses. "Our little town doesn't have much crime. We hardly have a police force. It could be a long wait. You might want to make coffee."

"Good idea. I'll go find the coffee in the kitchen. I need to calm my nerves," Grace said and then leaned close to my ear. "Remember, we're not in Florida anymore, where magic and paranormal are more accepted. Try to keep it, um, normal."

"Normal? We're witches in a Christmas-themed inn, with a dead person who could be mistaken for an elf. Oh, and there's a pig living here," I turned and replied to Grace's retreating form as she disappeared through a doorway. "Be careful!"

Jasper crept over to me. "Good luck with the whole keeping it normal thing."

I approached Arthur as he padded through the

lobby. He leaned heavily on a cane, clutching it with a gnarled hand, and seemed unfazed by the body and the pig. Arthur looked like he needed someone to care for him rather than he for the inn.

"I'm Grace's friend, Marissa," I said when he stopped to catch his breath. "Are you okay? Did you know the victim?"

"Takes a lot to surprise me at my age." He leaned toward the body. "Yep. I've seen him around. One of the new fellas we hired to help get the place ready for Grace. Think his name was Stuart? Or maybe Steve? Could've fallen over and hit his head? Or perhaps someone had it out for him. Few people working here most of the time. Would've been easy to get him alone."

My eyes widened. "Why would someone want to hurt him?"

Arthur shrugged. "Beats me."

He seemed satisfied with his rationale and toddled off to the kitchen as if deaths occurred here every day. Which made me want to ask Grace if she knew if other murders had happened here.

Jasper tilted his head to the side, gesturing that I should follow him to the hall. "The pig's name is Wilber. So far he's got nothing to say except to inform me he's upset that a cat—and a dog—are in what he considers *his* house." He rolled his eyes.

If the police were mortal, they wouldn't consider the paranormal aspects of the scene that could contribute to the cause of death. Those could make a murder look like an accident to a mortal. "Do you think the pig, Wilber, saw what happened?"

Jasper nodded. "Perhaps, but he's not talking about it."

It surprised me that Jasper could communicate with him at all. He claimed he couldn't communicate with Mulder. It was possible Jasper said he could talk to the pig since Mulder found the body and he wanted to be more of a part of whatever this was. "Well, you tried. Let's plan to meet the rest of the staff when they arrive. We can observe their reactions before the police get here."

Jasper perked up. Most people didn't think twice about what they said and did in front of a cat, especially when I didn't share about our ability to converse. This enabled Jasper to excel in gathering clues.

Most likely, this had been an accident, but I had a suspicious nature. Each time I thought I knew all there was to know about the paranormal, I discovered something new. For example, it wasn't long ago that I met my first real, live angel.

The door to the kitchen swung inward, and Grace stepped out. I stopped her before she could turn away after handing me a cup of nirvana, which most refer to as coffee. "I would've thought Arthur would've been more disturbed by the dead elf."

Grace pierced me with a look. "If you're looking for something to take your mind off the upcoming holidays, I can think of better things than imagining an accidental death into a murder."

She had a point. It may have been an accident, and I welcomed a distraction from this overabundance of Christmas, but not at the price of poor Stuart... or Steve's life. The first order of business needed to be confirming his name. It was bad enough the poor little man had to die in a forest of poinsettias.

2

Jasper, Grace, and I settled on the couch to face the lobby entrance and wait for the rest of the staff. Two armchairs flanked the area with a round wooden coffee table in the center. Mulder lingered in the kitchen, hoping for tidbits of food.

Sabina was the second staff member to arrive and provided the expected gasp of horror upon realizing there was a dead body in the lobby.

Although, her response might've been partially due to her being the housekeeper. We'd used a clean sheet from the linen closet to cover the body, which resulted in destroying more poinsettias. And it *still* didn't completely conceal the large red stain spread across the floor.

The one other thing we learned from Sabina,

besides her secret for folding a fitted sheet, was the correct name of the victim. It was Steve.

"The name doesn't fit an elf," I whispered to Grace, which got me an elbow to the side. Someday I'd learn not to share these thoughts.

"Steve had been assigned the night shift," Sabina said. "He was the only staff member working overnight. We've not had many guests, except for one —Belinda. She was here last night and is a regular who makes very few demands." Sabina cast her eyes to the covered body and trembled. "This is terrible. Very terrible."

"You let a guest stay at the inn alone?" I asked.

Sabina shrugged while regarding me. "Not me. Glenda made that decision. Besides, Belinda practically lives here. She thought it would be helpful to have someone stay overnight to monitor the place with Mid gone, but obviously, this did not help Steve."

The front door slammed. Grace and I started and turned to look, but Sabina remained unfazed. "That would be Glenda," she said before scurrying away.

Glenda stomped into the lobby. Her gaze darted to the covered corpse and then away.

I stood and held out my hand, "Hello, I'm—"

"What is going on?" The tall, thin woman started

spewing complaints while avoiding looking at the poinsettias.

Grace and I locked gazes and then nodded with an unspoken agreement to wait until Glenda wound down. People dealt with grief and tragedy in different ways. Sometimes it was best to let their emotions play out...or wait until they had a few cocktails in them. At least that was how I handled it at work in the club.

Most of Glenda's complaints were regarding the condition Steve had left the lobby in. These seemed unreasonable, since Steve wasn't simply lying down on the job and wouldn't care about having his pay docked or receiving a poor reference.

Glenda then made demands of Grace regarding whether she had decided to keep or sell the inn. Despite trying, and failing, to interrupt, I couldn't determine what her position was. Arthur had referred to her as an event planner and said she handled reservations, but she was the least likely person to work in customer service I'd ever seen. No wonder the inn only had one guest.

Grace sighed and sank further into the couch cushions, occasionally blurting out an apology for things that weren't her fault. Why Grace believed she was responsible for anything at an inn she'd just inherited, especially for how Glenda felt Grace had neglected rectifying a list of issues, was beyond me. Poor Grace was usually an upbeat person, but even she was unprepared to deal with Glenda's onslaught of unhappiness.

Glenda let out a screech, causing Mulder and Jasper to make themselves scarce and making me slosh coffee over the rim of my mug as I jumped to my feet. Had the killer decided to return? I scanned the room but only noted that Wilber had sprawled out in front of the fireplace. "What is it? The pig?"

"A dog! He might scare Sparkles." Glenda pointed to where Mulder peeked out from behind the coffee table.

"Who?" I asked.

"Mid's cat. I don't see her anywhere. She's probably hiding. That dog scared her," Glenda said. She rushed around the lobby and called for the cat. Wilber squealed and hurried into the hall as she approached.

I settled back into the couch, and Jasper slunk behind it, close enough so I could hear his continued requests for breakfast but hidden from Glenda's view.

"Good morning!" The lone guest said as she descended the stairs to the lobby.

After we pressed her for her story, Belinda insisted she'd slept soundly through the ordeal. She confessed to taking sleeping pills and washing them down with a glass of wine—not a recommended combination, but apparently an effective one if you wanted to sleep through anything.

I was trying to say something in between Glenda's complaining and Grace's apologies when Belinda intervened by grabbing the staircase banister and announcing, "A man is dead."

Her comment, or perhaps the way she lay her palm across her brow and swooned in a theatrical manner, brought a hush over the room, even stopping Jasper's incessant complaints about the meal he'd missed, which was a real accomplishment.

It could've been the way Belinda stood so majestically, or the dramatic way she said the words, but one thing was for sure: when she talked, people listened—for a limited time, until she began fussing over Wilber.

"There's my boy. I wondered where you'd gone to," she said while patting his head. His corkscrew tail wagged along with his behind at her affections. She attached a harness. As they walked past to go outside, the jingle bells adorning the leash chimed with each step of his hooves.

Grace stood and smoothed her hands over her pants. "She's right. The situation has us all upset. I wish the police would get here. I'm going to see if there's anything I can do in the kitchen."

Another woman walked through the main entrance as Belinda and Wilber exited. She sidled up beside me.

I extended my hand. “Hi, I'm Marissa.”

“Hello! I'm Janice, the realtor,” she said with a bright smile.

When Janice took my hand, I said, “I'm not sure Grace has decided whether she wants to sell. This isn't a good time.”

My poor friend had enough on her mind without being barraged by the realtor.

Janice retrieved her hand from my grip and nodded. “I heard. News travels faster than the police around here.” Her eyes widened. The color rising in her cheeks matched the large pink flowers on her dress. “A dead body? That’s awful. Just awful. I was already on my way to bring Grace a welcome bag.” She held up a plastic gift bag with a Beauty Bits logo on it. “Nothing like a little pampering to raise a woman’s spirits.”

The realtor smelled mortal. From what Grace had shared, her aunt Mid didn't hide being a witch; on the contrary, she flaunted the fact. Surely Janice understood her beauty products could never hold a candle to what many witches could create themselves. “Like I said, it’s not a good time.”

My comment may have come out harsher than I’d

intended, but I was tired. The last thing we needed was people from town showing up to gather gossip.

"They're just free samples." Janice gave me a once-over and appeared to not be too pleased with what she saw. "Are you always so outspoken?"

"Usually." Especially when I wanted to protect my friends from pushy realtors.

Janice tilted her head and studied me. "Then you won't mind me suggesting a color rinse to get rid of the black strands you overlooked when you colored your hair."

"No, I do mind, and I don't color my hair." It wasn't quite a lie; Joe, my hairstylist did any coloring. But not for the reason this mortal woman thought. My lack of spelling finesse often showed. A black streak occurred with a spell gone awry, but the stubborn one Janice had fixed her gaze on had appeared when a charmed cocktail had exploded. It had left me with the ability to communicate with Jasper, and a black streak that refused to budge.

The heavy foundation on Janice's cheeks strained when she plastered on her yellowed-teeth saleswoman smile. "Fine." She handed me the bag. "Please give this to Grace. I think *she* will appreciate the products."

Janice nodded and then left.

I sat back down on the couch. A few moments

later Grace returned from the kitchen to sit beside me. I placed my hand on her shoulder. "I'm sorry this trip isn't starting out like you expected. Here, this is from the realtor, Janice." I handed her the bag of beauty products.

The plastic crinkled as Grace accepted the bag, then set it beside her on the couch. "Honestly, I wasn't sure what to expect when we arrived, but this wasn't it." She took in the room. "My memories here were happy ones. So much has changed since I was here last."

The jingling bells on Wilber's harness announced his and Belinda's return.

"Like having a pig for a guest?" I raised my brows. My comment drew a smile from Grace. "Don't you find it odd that Belinda stays at the inn so much?"

Grace glanced at Belinda, who was currently tying a holiday-themed bib around Wilber's neck. "I think her desire to stay here is one of the least odd things about the whole situation," she said. "She's having repairs done to her house and says she likes the atmosphere here. At least we have one guest."

I wasn't sure if her reference to the atmosphere meant old and disintegrating, or the ancient Christmas decorations. Most likely, it was because no one else would let Belinda's pig have the run of the place—or allow him indoors. Grace had never been a take-charge kind of witch and preferred to avoid confrontation to keep the peace. I suspected Wilber wouldn't be evicted if she kept the inn.

"Should we go over and say something else to the staff about Steve? At least offer our condolences?" Grace ran her hand over her eyes. "I feel so helpless."

"Have you ever met an elf?" I threw out the question to distract her from dwelling on our current situation. Part of me really wanted her to say she had. My disdain for the Christmas holiday had started when other kids mocked me for clinging to what many considered to be childish beliefs for years longer than most.

"An elf? I don't know. I can't say I ever met one," Grace said.

The small glimmer of hope squelched within me. I wouldn't go through that humiliation again. Beliefs of elves, Santa, and flying reindeer were stories for children, not for an adult witch who should know better.

Finally, a police officer arrived in the small lobby. "It took him long enough," I said. The casual attire didn't confirm the man's profession, but the flash of a badge clipped to the waist of his pants and the collective sigh of relief from the staff did.

I stood. "Finally, someone who can confirm that this is a crime scene."

"We don't know that yet, Marissa. Don't jump to conclusions. It's like you look for trouble." Grace closed her eyes and leaned back against the cushion.

A response was unnecessary; Grace knew I excelled at jumping to conclusions, and I couldn't help it that trouble usually found me.

It relieved me to have someone taking charge of the situation. Even though I'd been key in solving several other crimes—which Jasper took credit for—I wasn't confident in determining the next steps of the process. I was also happy Glenda could complain to someone else besides me. She had depleted my little remaining energy after a long night of driving with no sleep.

Truth be told, if he'd arrived in uniform, I might've thought someone was about to turn on the music. With tight jeans, dark wavy hair, high cheekbones, and a muscled body barely concealed under his heavy jacket, he'd provide an engaging dance show for a birthday or bachelorette party.

I was immune to his charms after coming off a recent relationship that ended before it got started. Still, there weren't many men who could hold a candle to an angel.

The police officer seemed used to the attention and got right to business by going directly to Grace and extending his hand. "Hello, I'm Officer Klaus."

Grace grasped his hand in both of her own, and her smile could melt butter. "Thank you for coming. This is such a tragedy. Call me Grace, please."

"Grace. A perfect name for the new owner of our lovely Kringle Inn," he said with a smile. "Wait. Grace Starley? I haven't seen you since we were kids when you used to visit."

Grace gasped. "Nick. I can't believe it. You're all grown up."

The snort escaped before I could stop myself. He shot me a narrowed gaze and Grace's eyes widened. She should be used to my outbursts and should've expected a reaction to his unusual name from me.

"No, I ... surely you get it. Nick Klaus? Really? At the Kringle Inn? Who just drove up from Tinsel Town? To investigate the death of a dead man who looks like an elf?" My laugh faded as both of them stared at me like I was the most insensitive person in the world. I glanced at Grace. She knew me well enough to know I often handled uncomfortable situations with sarcasm or inappropriate laughter. I couldn't help myself, but when you're friends with me, you get the complete package of characteristics —the good, the bad, and the embarrassing.

Now all Grace had eyes for was for Mr. Klaus. It was easy to see why. He was the polar opposite of the white-bearded, rotund man of his namesake, and not old at all. He was probably in the perfect age range for Grace.

But Grace was flirting at a time like this? Fatigue must have been catching up with her. And based on Nick's scent, he was one-hundred percent mortal. Nick might need someone paranormal to help with looking into the death, whether or not he admitted it.

3

"I'm sorry, Nick. Don't mind Marissa. She's just upset. We had a long night of driving. Then to arrive to find poor Steve," Grace stumbled over her words, and then shot me a look. "I also neglected to mention the theme of the inn, which was a shock for someone who has no love for Christmas and holiday decorations."

"Nonsense," I said. There was no reason to share my dislike of the décor. My avoidance of the season was comparable to a vamp and the sun. Gran had encouraged me to accompany Grace, making me wonder if she'd been privy to this tidbit of information. She'd been trying to get me to shed my disdain for the holiday for years. But the older I got, the less magic it held. It felt more like an overabundance of consumerism and a never-ending to-do list. "The red just clashes with my hair."

I patted my pink tresses. That much was true. My boss at the Night Moves club in Florida, Vlad, pushed the Christmas theme to sell more drink specials and made our already uncomfortable uniform more embarrassing by adding a holiday hat. The Santa hat didn't go well with my coloring, although the occasional hat was helpful to hide streaks incurred from any magical mishaps.

"Never mind. Please accept my apologies," I said, trying to cut through his glare. I extended my hand. "I'm Marissa."

"We have a grinch in our midst?" Nick kept a hold of my hand as he studied me with a narrowed gaze. "A holiday hater? A bah-humbugger?"

"A what? Don't be ridiculous. Besides, the dead man in the poinsettias is a more relevant concern than whether I love the holiday season." I pulled my hand back and gestured to the area, noting more people had arrived. Belinda had appointed herself to steering them away from the lobby and the body as if she owned the place. If there were clues to be found, they wouldn't be here for long. "This place is filling up faster than a clown car," I said. 'Who are all these other people besides those working the crime scene?"

"We're still not sure it's a crime scene." Grace

followed my gaze. "Oh, and Arthur said there were more maintenance workers arriving today."

I swallowed my retort about their elf-like resemblance to Steve, knowing I'd get no support from these two. If they weren't elves, or something of the like, I'd strongly recommend Grace ensure the inn would not get stuck with a discrimination case if they only hired little people and made them dress like elves.

"Although this appears to be an accident, I need to do my job, ladies." He turned to Grace. "Let me know if there's anything you need."

"Thank you." Grace dipped her head and studied him from under her lashes.

As I turned to walk away, I felt a hand on my shoulder. "And you. Don't be going too far," Nick said in an authoritative tone.

I frowned. "What's that supposed to mean? Where am I going to go except maybe to get lost in the cold candy land surrounding the inn? No, thank you. I've gotten too accustomed to the warm weather of Florida." Perhaps Officer Nick had realized I might be an asset in helping solve the case. "Unless you want me to lend a hand with the investigation and securing the scene?"

"That won't be necessary. I meant you need to

stick around because I might have more questions for you," Nick replied without a trace of humor.

"For me? Why?" I stepped back and almost trampled Jasper where he sat cleaning his paws. Hygiene was high on his list of priorities. Not even death or delayed meals would deter him from his daily routine.

Nick shoved his hands in his pockets. "Because you found the body. I don't know you, but I *do* know you're a real bah-humbug and you're staying at the Kringle Inn."

This turn of events didn't surprise Jasper, who muttered, "Of course he suspects you; why not? Why would the only person who can hear me not be in line to blame for every oddball crime?"

"A bah-humbug? That's what I'm guilty of?" I shook my head. "That's ridiculous. You're saying I'm a person of interest because I don't care about the holiday?"

It was fruitless to point out that I hadn't found the body. Mulder did. My bad luck had accompanied me north.

Grace was either too tired from the events of the day or didn't want to alienate Nick to offer any support.

"Fine. I'm going to look around," I said.

Nick glanced at Jasper. "Cute, pudgy cat, you got there."

"Pudgy? Who is he calling pudgy?" Jasper hissed at me. "I don't like him either. We'll solve the case without Romeo here."

Nick reached down to pet Jasper, but the cat ducked from his touch. He called after me, "Touch nothing in the lobby until I'm done examining the scene."

"No problem." I'd give Mr. Bigger-than-his-britches space to do his job. I'd seen more bodies in a month than he had all year in this holly jolly Christmas town.

I wandered from the lobby down the hall, past the obnoxious light display and plethora of decorations lining the narrow hallway of the ancient-looking inn. I paused. One wall was covered with framed photographs and paintings of various guests from over the years.

"Finally, something that's not Christmas," I said. Everyone appeared happy in the pictures. The present staff seemed drained of their holiday spirit. Whether it was from the gradual fading of the inn, Mid's death, and now Steve, remained to be determined.

On our drive here, Grace had shared memories of her visits in her youth, though she neglected to mention the overwhelming Christmas theme. I imagined this wasn't what she'd expected. The place falling apart at the seams, one lone guest with her pig, and a dead body.

This certainly wasn't an ideal October getaway.

I stopped at a photo that had to have been Grace's aunt. Her features matched Grace's, and she had the same sparkle of kindness in her eyes and a ready, open smile. The resemblance ended there.

Grace was conservative, so most didn't suspect she was capable of powerful magic. She could quietly blend into a crowd, while Mid's picture screamed, *Look at me, I'm a witch!* From the photo, her Aunt Mid seemed to embrace everything about life.

Elevated into one of those old beehive styles, her hair had a pointed hat perched on top. Her tresses were a shocking pink—more so than mine, and that was saying something. The style and color made it resemble cotton candy. I might describe the brightly colored clothes as being flamboyant. She leaned on the handle of a broom. Her mouth was open, and her eyes were twinkling, like the camera had caught her in the middle of a laugh. "She looks like a piece of candy."

Mulder had followed me over and was observing my inspection of the photograph. When I mentioned candy, his tail began wagging. "Sorry, buddy. I don't have anything. This woman looks like she's candy in the flesh." I wiped my hand over the picture frame. A small gold plaque on the frame dated it a few decades ago. From what I could gather from the décor in the photo, they took it before the place started the slow decline into near demise. It must've killed Mid to see the inn crumbling into its current state.

I frowned. Perhaps it literally had killed her? Two dead people in one old inn in a short time. I turned to Mulder, who continued to wiggle and wait for the promised candy yet to materialize. "Coincidence? I don't believe in coincidences. Do you?"

Mulder let out a low whine, which was probably related to my continued questions instead of offering him something edible.

I placed my hands on my hips and turned to study the scene in the lobby. "Well, at least we'll have something to keep us occupied during our visit. Finding out who's responsible for these murders."

AFTER I TOOK A NAP, I FOUND GRACE UNPACKING. It had taken me longer than expected to locate her room—cheerfully titled as Sleigh Bells—since the explosion of old, faded Christmas decorations and themes for every room had me going in circles.

The police officer's comments about me churned through my thoughts.

I started talking as I entered her room. "Don't worry, Grace. I'll get to the bottom of these murders. We both know I had nothing to do with it. *Rusty cauldrons*, we just got here. Does the man think I can time travel? He's a mortal and probably doesn't believe in magic, unless it's the magic of the Christmas season." I spoke the last words with heavy sarcasm and tossed my hands up.

Grace paused from folding a shirt. "For one, I don't know what murders you're talking about. Steve had an unfortunate accident. For two, if there is anything to look into, I'm sure Nick will."

"It's Nick already, huh? What do you think about Officer Klaus?" I emphasized his full title and then held up my hand when Grace got all misty-eyed. "Besides how he looks. What I mean is, do you think he's going to take this seriously?"

I meant investigating Steve's death, but part of me also wondered if he seriously thought I might be a suspect. As if I despised the holiday season so much that I'd show up and take out the first person I saw because they reminded me of a Christmas elf. That was crazy. I wasn't a killer. Besides, the children's taunts of how elves weren't real still echoed in my mind from my childhood.

Grace contemplated my question as she lined up her neatly folded clothes on the edge of the bed.

"Well, he took his time doing a thorough investigation of the scene, and he talked to each of the staff and Belinda."

"Did he interview Wilber?" I sat on the bed, admitting to myself that the rooms were adorable. Old, outdated, and in desperate need of updating, but delightful. Even the holiday theme and decorations weren't too bad. The inn might grow on me.

"Who?" Grace furrowed her brow.

"You couldn't miss him. Corkscrew tail, eats anything. You know, the pig."

Grace laughed. "Don't be ridiculous. Besides, not everyone can talk to animals like you can."

"I can only talk to my cat." I slid down to lay on my side on her bed, propping my head up with my palm. "I'm only looking at all the potential suspects. I gotta help Nick rule out the possibility that a Christmas-hater like me was responsible."

"I think he was kidding about that." Grace tugged at one handle on the old chest of drawers until the drawer relented with a creak and opened. She began placing her clothing inside in orderly stacks. "I don't suppose you've unpacked yet."

Grace knew the answer without me having to respond. Back in my room, my clothing was overflowing from my suitcase where I'd dug through it. I also didn't ask if assigning me to the A Christmas

Carol room was intentional. Perhaps she hoped I'd be visited by three ghosts to change my perspective while I was here—or because she thought I was a scrooge.

This trip was supposed to be fun, but so far, not so much. The tense expression was foreign on Grace's face. It was time for an intervention. "Are you thinking what I'm thinking?"

"I doubt it, but first you'll have to share what you're thinking." She zipped the suitcase closed and shoved it under the bed.

"How about one of my specialty cocktails?" When Grace grimaced, I hurried to add, "I can make you a virgin one."

"When you say virgin, do you mean one without alcohol or one without your extra ingredients?" She raised a brow.

"Without alcohol, of course. The charmed ingredients are the whole point of my cocktails. Otherwise, they aren't special." I was exceptional at creating drinks. It was my specialty cocktails, which were infused with a bit of magic, that were a hit or a miss. Usually, it was nothing more serious than indigestion, but I couldn't deny combining charms and cocktails wasn't always my strong point. That didn't deter me from my goal of becoming a stellar mixologist of witch-charmed drinks.

"I'll pass."

"Hey, I'm getting better. Suit yourself. I'll have to check out the ingredients available here." I took in the room. "This whole place is like something from Santa's Village." If there only was a real Santa's village, I added to myself.

Grace sighed. "It used to look better. I can't believe how much it's deteriorated. Now I feel bad about how long it's been since I visited. Especially since Mid didn't have any children. She had the staff, and the entire town, as her family. Everyone loved her."

I raised a brow. "Maybe not one person."

Grace laid her hairbrush on the dresser and turned to me. "Every death isn't a murder. Just because you came across a few bodies before, doesn't make you a detective, or require the need to think everything is related to foul play."

"That's true. Most times, a death isn't the result of foul play. I want to give Steve's death, and maybe Mid's, the benefit of the doubt." I sat up on the bed. The mattress sagged toward the floor.

Grace ignored my comment. Before Nick left, he hadn't declared it a murder scene, that I know of anyway. Although, I wasn't sure how the process worked. Most of my knowledge about police procedure came from television shows.

There was yellow crime scene tape around the area in the lobby, but someone had added twinkly lights to it to make it look like it was part of the décor. I was pretty sure this wasn't procedure.

The holiday photo on the wall near Grace's bed had a small switch on the side. I clicked it and the lights around the farmhouse in the picture flashed. "You've seen the place. Except for finding a body on arrival, what do you think? Sell it, or keep the inn?" I asked.

Part of me desperately wanted Grace to say she was going to sell it. Then she wouldn't be living states away from me. But another part of me knew Grace might enjoy being an innkeeper. She'd been bouncing around more jobs than I had been, trying to find what fit her best. As a witch whose attitude and spells were always full of optimism and light, this might be the perfect job for her. Everyone loved her —just another thing she had in common with her Aunt Mid.

"Honestly? I haven't decided yet." Grace took in the room, homing in on the peeling wallpaper in the corner. "It needs work."

"You have a handy person here. Well, you have an entire crew of them." I said. Perhaps the staff had been trying to get the place up to par to impress Grace and get her to keep the inn, although

I hated to think how it had looked before they'd started.

Grace's smile was full of mischief. "And I have you to help me get the decorations looking fabulous."

I covered my face with my hands. "You're kidding, right?"

4

Jasper hopped up and got way too close to my face, almost crossing his almond-shaped eyes to pin them on mine. "There are more pressing things to discuss than holiday decorations." He sat back on his haunches. "Although, I enjoy batting around a decorative bulb or two. But please, lay off the tinsel. That stuff is irresistibly delicious." He made a face. "But the aftereffects on the digestive system can be quite unpleasant."

I tried to inch away, but not before Jasper's whiskers tickled my cheek. "You're the only one who might be interested in eating tinsel. You, or perhaps, Wilber. Belinda said he'll eat anything."

Grace glanced from me to the cat and then resumed unpacking another suitcase. She was one of the few people who knew about my ability to communicate with Jasper, and it was nice to have someone who accepted you as you were.

Jasper sat back and began licking his paw. “That's what I came here to talk to you about. The pig. Wilber. You distracted me with this talk of decorations.”

“What about Wilber?” I asked. “Did he say something about what happened to Steve?”

“He hasn't said a word except that he wants me and the ‘log of fur with googly eyes’ to vacate the premises.” He glanced down to where Mulder was curled up on the floor. “Sorry, big boy—his words, not mine. Not that you couldn't stand to lose a pound or two.” He returned his focus to me. “Personally, I think the pig could be responsible. He’s not very nice.”

“Really, Marissa,” Grace said once Jasper quieted. “I think you're overthinking this. Steve fell and hit his head. It's awful, but every death isn’t a murder.”

I sat up and smoothed my unruly curls. “Every one I’ve come across usually was...Well, at least lately.”

Grace put her hands on her hips. “You do hang around some unsavory people. Perhaps that's part of the problem.”

“I hang around you,” I said.

"That's different. I mean the people at the club where you work. The place draws a dangerous crowd."

"When you have a demon bartender, I guess that's the crowd you might get." I shrugged, but Grace didn't see it since she was heading toward the door.

"I'm going to talk to Glenda." Grace's expression mimicked that of biting into a lemon when she said the name. "I need to find out what shape this place is in. It will help me decide what I want to do. While I'm gone, you can think about how to improve the decorations."

I groaned.

Jasper said, "I'd rather think about anything else than holiday decorations." Then he jumped off the bed.

I stared down at my cat, who was busy peering under the bed, most likely looking for dust bunnies or other odds and ends a guest may have lost. "You know, while I was exploring, I stopped to talk with Sabina..."

Jasper glanced up at me and then returned his attention to under the bed. "How? Her mixture of Cajun and English makes it difficult to understand anything. Although, you humans always talk like your mouth is full of marbles."

"Hey, I can understand you, right?" When he

ignored me, I pressed on: "Anyway, it seems her great grandmother is some kind of voodoo priestess, and Sabina remembers a few of her spells."

"*That* just happened to come up in conversation? Like you don't have enough trouble with garden variety spells, let alone something mixing in voodoo. You'd end up with your hair coal black before the end of the week, and you don't have Joe around to fix it."

"This is different. I might excel at this type of magic," I said. "Voodoo is something different and new." Jasper growled in protest when I reached to scoop him up. I darted across the hall with him in tow and set him beside me on the bed in my room.

"What are you doing? I've told you I hate it when you pick me up. It's very undignified and rude," Jasper snarled.

"You weren't paying attention to me," I said. "This is important."

"I was. You don't require one hundred percent of my concentration. Besides, you were talking nonsense about voodoo spells, or potions, or whatnot. What does that have to do with me?"

I smiled. "Plenty. You're going to love this idea."

Jasper cocked his head. "You saying that makes me sure I will *not* love it. In fact, I think I'll hate it."

"I asked Sabina if she saw or heard anything unusual before the murder—"

"No one said it was a murder. Yet." Jasper studied me with an uneasy expression. He might've been a great sidekick in getting information, but he never liked my ideas when they involved magic.

"She told me how to do a spell. It's called a second eye spy." I clapped my hands together.

"Why would you trust her? If she knows voodoo magic, she might have murdered Steve and fear you suspect her. This spell could incapacitate you. Then you could be her next victim," he said, his almond-shaped eyes widening. "Did you tell her about your skills, or should I say, lack of, for magic spells? How do you know it's not a curse? Or a hex? You're liable to end up with a third eye in the middle of your forehead."

I waved a hand at him, feigning more confidence than I felt about her innocence. Everyone would be a suspect until I proved them innocent—or I tired of determining if there had truly been a murder. It was better than contemplating the Christmas holidays when it wasn't Halloween yet. "It's nothing like that. The spell provides a way to ride along with someone and see and hear what they see. Like a little spy."

"What do you mean by a ride along? If you're referring to me, which I'm guessing by the look in your two current eyes, I can tell you it will not work.

You're," he raked his gaze over me, "many, many times my size."

"Not in person, silly. I would ride along in your mind."

Jasper let out a hiss and jumped to the floor, backing away with his tail raised. "In my mind? What kind of hocus pocus are you getting into? Most likely, it wouldn't work. With your lackluster spelling abilities, you could end up trapped there, and that wouldn't be good for anyone. Who would remember to feed me?"

"Enough of the insults about my spelling." Most of them were true, but I was practicing and getting better. Potions were more my thing. Well, they were getting to be my thing. "It's not an evil spell, so I shouldn't get more black streaks in my hair."

"I'm not worried about your hair. Besides, there's nothing wrong with black hair. Feast your eyes on my glorious fur." He swished his tail from side-to-side.

"Yes, you're lovely, whatever. Now, listen. I know this spell sounds far-fetched, but it could be fun."

"Nope, not fun at all. Zero fun. Nada." He kept backing away toward the door.

"But I thought you wanted to be my familiar?" It was low of me to play that card, but I knew how to sway him to my favor.

Jasper stopped and remained silent for a moment

as he considered it. "I don't see how that matters in this situation."

"Our bond could grow stronger with a spell like this. Who knows? You might gain some magic yourself." I did not know if any of this was true.

He paused and lowered his tail. "You're joking."

"No, I've heard it could happen. I can't guarantee it would, but it's possible. If anything were to go wrong, Grace is here. She could fix it."

Jasper nodded. "That much I can agree on. Grace is much better at spelling than you'll ever be, and I've never seen one dark strand in her hair."

I clapped my hands together. "We can find out much more about everyone this way."

"You mean *you* can. Obviously, this is how I always find out things. You're just jealous you don't have my stealth and want it for yourself. There are benefits to being small."

I stood from the bed and grabbed my oversized purse. "Let's get started."

"Now?" Jasper's eyes widened.

I stopped digging in the bottomless pit that was my purse. "Why not? We can try to approach Wilber again."

"What, and get stomped on with one of his cloven hoofs, or mixed into his dinner trough?"

I waved him off. "I can help you with finessing the

conversation. I already have all the ingredients gathered here in my purse, so let's get ready."

"You were optimistic that I was going to agree to this spell, I see." Jasper leapt on the bed. "Elevated to the role of familiar, you say?"

"Maybe? I knew you'd see my side." I laid out a small bowl and the ingredients, including the one item Sabina insisted was essential. I had to make it myself to personalize it to the spell. With limited time and supplies available for crafting, it wasn't perfect.

"What in the tuna is that?" Jasper shrieked.

"This?" I knew the tiny homemade voodoo cat doll might push him over the edge. "It's nothing. The figure helps to make sure this works right and that I end up in the correct person's thoughts that we intended the spell for."

Mulder came stumbling into the room, falling over his feet on the slippery floor and taking a nose-dive. He came to a stop with a skittering of paws at the foot of the bed. His irritated huffs and raised behind confirmed that he'd discovered something of interest under the bed.

Jasper studied me with a wary expression. "Don't you think we need to tell Grace what we're doing here first?"

I shrugged and sat on the bed. "She's busy. No need to worry her. Besides, what could go wrong?"

"DID IT WORK?" I LOOKED AROUND—MY VIEW WAS about a foot from the ground. "It must've worked! Jasper? Can you hear me? If you can hear me, say something." There was no response, but I was definitely not in my usual form. Besides the close view of the floor, everything felt odd. Like I was floating.

We were moving. A quick turn of his head gave me a view of under the bed and what had held Mulder's attention. A shiny earring someone must've lost lay forgotten, along with a few dust bunnies. Perhaps Grace should have a word with Sabina about upkeep of the rooms. It shouldn't be difficult with such few guests.

"Jasper? Say something."

Perhaps he couldn't hear me, but I was getting the world from a cat's eye view. "Cool." Hopefully, I could figure out how to guide him and we could investigate together.

He stopped and turned toward the full-length mirror on the closet door.

"Holy cannoli!" I came face to furry face with—

Mulder. I wasn't hitching a ride in Jasper's thoughts. I was in Mulder's. This definitely wasn't part of my plan, and as far as I knew, we couldn't communicate the same way.

"Mulder!"

He stopped panting and stared into the mirror, looking more perplexed than usual. I might not be able to communicate with him as I'd planned with Jasper, but it seemed like Mulder could hear me. Perhaps I could get mileage out of this spell after all.

He started toward the door and then stopped to peer up at the bed at Jasper. My dog may or may not understand the cat, but even in this form, I could. I saw myself sitting on the bed, cross-legged, with my eyes closed as I performed the spell.

That was weird.

"This is priceless! Enjoy your ride-along with Sir Poops-A-Lot. Hope you're feeling optimistic about this spell now." Jasper collapsed on his back in a fit of laughter.

"I'm glad you're amused by this," I said. Jasper continued laughing as if he couldn't hear me, or didn't care to respond, since he was too busy laughing.

Mulder had to have heard my voice, because he spun to the mirror again as if his image had sassed him. He had a confused expression, making him appear like he was considering whether he needed to go to the bathroom.

"Go downstairs, Mulder," I shouted in my mind.

Nothing.

He continued to sit there, staring from the mirror to my body on the bed, appearing to contemplate why my voice was in his head while my eyes were closed and my mouth wasn't moving.

I needed to get him out of this room to take advantage of this mishap and investigate. Who knew how long the spell would last.

"Go get your toy. Get your toy! Get your toy!" I elevated my voice in the sing-song manner many used when talking to babies, and it was how I talked to Mulder. It was working.

Mulder wiggled and shimmied with excitement at the thought of getting his toy. I'd only brought a few along for the trip, so it ought to take him time to search for them and allow me to do some snooping.

He exited into the hall, peered around, and found it empty. I gasped when a loud voice filled my head.

"*Finally, a break from that ridiculous cat. I don't know what Mistress Marissa sees in the annoying fur ball. He has about as much sense as the dust bunnies that hold his attention for so long. What a nincompoop.*

"*Get your toy—please! Like we both don't know she didn't bring but one or two, and not my most favorite toys.*

That's probably for the best, with that pig around. He'd probably jump at the chance to mess with my things. I can only hope Mistress Marissa doesn't think I'll share any of the toys she's surely procured for me for the vacation with this beast."

"Mulder?"

5

"Mulder? Is that you?" Was I hearing his thoughts?

He stopped. Slight surrounding sounds increased as his ears perked up and he gazed around.

I must've been. It differed from how I communicated with Jasper because we actually seemed to converse. This spell was more invasive.

I'd invaded his thoughts and totally confused the dog. It was shocking to grasp that my silly dog with the attention span of a gnat, who appeared to have the intellect of a kindergartener, might be much smarter than I'd realized.

After a moment of brief hesitation, Mulder shook. His ears flopped against his head and the quivering proceeded down his body and exited through his tail. The movement felt like I'd endured a minor earthquake.

He trotted down the hall.

I'd neglected to ask Sabina how long the spell would last. Hopefully, I could still benefit from the situation, even with the unintended consequences of now being able to hear my dog's thoughts. "Mulder. It's me, Mistress Marissa."

I used the term he addressed me with, hoping to get his attention. He spun around, jerking his head in every direction to pinpoint the location of my voice.

The movement and rushing scenery made me dizzy. You could sure take in a lot at once with his enormous eyes. I guess that was why he never seemed to miss anything.

"*Who in tarnation is toying with me now? I don't have time for these silly games. Now that Miss Marissa, and that feline, are otherwise occupied, I must get to the kitchen. Perhaps I can finally get some decent food. If the pig beats me there, I'll be lucky if I get the usual slop and leftovers. These newbies in the Inn are fair game to my adorableness. They'll understand my need for sustenance.*"

"Mulder, listen. It's me, Mama." I figured my only chance was to get it out all at once. Otherwise, all I'd gain for my troubles was a view of my dog inhaling mass quantities of food. "I did a spell because I wanted to find clues about the murder. I'm in your thoughts. We can work together on this. It will be our mission." I had to struggle not to use the singsong tone I usually did when I was trying to convince him to do something.

Mulder came to a stop. "*In my thoughts? Well, that's quite intrusive. Asking me first would've been nice.*"

"You believe me?" I thought I'd have to do more convincing once I got him to pay attention. His ready acceptance was surprising. "If I'd planned this, I would've asked you." I didn't point out I wouldn't have known what his answer was, even if I'd thought to ask permission. But I also didn't know I'd end up as a passenger in my dog's brain instead of my cat's. "The spell kind of has a mind of its own."

"*Now that, I believe. You have more magical mishaps than any of the witches I've met. Yet despite your frequent accidents, they do not make you feel shame, like some of us have had to endure.*"

"Um, sorry. I didn't realize there was another way to...err... train you."

"*Train? I need training? We know my breed is beloved by royalty and meant to be companions. You and I were doing fine until you brought that stray in. That cat thinks he's a big cheese since you can talk with him, but you've never tried to listen to me. We both know I should be your familiar. Tell him to abandon the thought.*"

Mulder sat at the top of the stairs, panting,

waiting for my response. I hadn't realized how much I might've hurt his feelings with the recent addition to our family. He always appeared amicable and happy-go-lucky. I suppose looks could be deceiving.

"I'm sorry. But now, at this moment, I can talk to you. I'm not sure how long this will last. Let's make this our little mission," I said.

"*Who are you calling little?*"

Despite Mulder being a tiny, stocky dog, he acted like he was a big brute when he knew I was there to have his back. If I wasn't nearby, it was a different story. All his bravado disintegrated faster than a pumpkin after Halloween.

"Not you, of course. You're my big boy. Come on, let's go snoop around and see if we can get any information."

"*About what? The scheduled meal times?*"

"No. About the murder. Or to determine if there was a murder."

"*Oh, there was a murder,*" Mulder huffed.

My breath caught in my currently nonexistent throat. "What do you mean? Did you hear or see something?"

"*Hear? See? You humans rely on the weakest of the senses. I smelled it. Dogs have an innate sense of detecting what occurred immediately before a death based on the smell. If the death is because of natural causes, it is a distinct scent. Different than when it's a murder. I learned that from the last dead body, which you gave full credit to Jasper for assisting you.*

You've never given me enough credit. You're too busy believing everything that fur ball tells you. Plus, there are the spirits to consider. They're never happy after being murdered. Some are downright furious about it." He shivered. "*Others are frightful and looking for justice, but helpless to find it. Often, I don't let on I can see them, but some of them, they know. Go ahead, ask Jasper. I'm sure he can help you by bumbling into something."*

"Again, apologies. Now, how do you know the little man ... I mean Steve, was murdered?"

"*It's not kind to make fun of people who are smaller than you. In fact, it's rude."*

I rolled my eyes since he wouldn't be aware of my expressions in his thoughts. Who'd have thought he was so sensitive? The dog had a perfect poker face. "Seriously, how many times do I have to apologize? If you want to help me out, spill the beans on this already. We can go to counseling or have long heart-to-heart talks later after we resolve this."

I probably had little time left before the spell stopped working. *If* it stopped working. With a shudder, I considered the consequences of being stuck in Mulder's thoughts forever if the spell had backfired.

"*You know I realize you're mocking me? And with your*

spelling history, there's a good chance you may never replicate this spell again. You're saying those things to placate me. But that's fine. I want justice as much as the next person."

I bit my nonexistent tongue when he referred to himself as a person. I'd always treated him like one, but obviously, he thought I didn't do enough. No response was necessary regarding his comment about the spell. That much was true. No need to validate it.

"*If you're so concerned about it, rest assured, Steve's death was accidental.*"

"But you said there was a murder. Do you mean a murder of a person?" Could Mulder tell the difference, since he considered himself a person? How did he tell time? He could refer to something that had happened to another animal at some point, or some time ago. We'd been here just a short time, and Steve was the only dead person I was aware of. Part of me wondered why I was putting so much faith in Mulder's opinions.

"*Of course, it was a person. It was Grace's beloved Aunt Mid.*"

I gasped as I opened my eyes. I was still sitting on the bed cross-legged, in the same position as when I'd started the spell. Jasper was curled up asleep beside me. Every part of my body was protesting from having stayed in this cramped position for an extended time.

A quick look confirmed that Mulder was nowhere to be seen. If I had actually been in his thoughts, then I could assume he was on his way to the kitchen.

The experience from the spell hadn't gone as I'd expected. Had I been in Mulder's mind? Had he told me Aunt Mid had been murdered? He'd given me this new information about her and Steve, but I didn't find out why he thought this. Plus, I had no experience with which to validate his impressions. He was adorable, but his cute appearance made him look like somewhat of a dizzy doofus.

I stretched out my legs, and Jasper rolled to his side and cracked one eye open. "Are you back? Or did you do one of those goofy trading places gigs where you're now living as a dog and Mulder can live in your body? Oh, my goddess; that would be amazing." He stood from his catnap and arched his back in a stretch. Then he raised his voice to mock the singsong tone I use when I talked to Mulder. "Here, let me test it out. *Do you want a treat? Want a treat?*"

"Enough. That's mean." Mulder never seemed to mind it, but maybe I didn't give him the respect he deserved.

Jasper laid his head on his paws and studied me. "That was epic to see you hitch a ride with the hound instead of me. It worked out perfectly. I got a nap, and you confirmed you shouldn't mess with unpredictable voodoo. Stick with potions." He paused. "Your success is a hit or miss even then."

"Guess what, Mr. Smarty Pants? It did work, and Mulder is smarter than you give him credit for. He had the information I needed. He said Steve's death was accidental and Aunt Mid was murdered."

Jasper's eyes widened. "And you believe this? Why? Because the dog told you? What evidence does he have? When has he ever provided us with any help in solving a case? He cannot be your familiar. You promised!"

Jasper's jealousy was clear, but he had a point about the lack of evidence.

"No one said anything about Mulder becoming my familiar. As far as what he said, I believe him," I said. "He's the most honest dog I know."

That much was true. Mulder immediately had to purge himself of guilt. Whether he'd chewed something up, or had a toileting accident, he would lead me to the crime scene and admit his guilt by lowering head, tucking his tail between his legs, and whining. Then he'd sit in agony until I forgave him.

"What did he say? How does he know this?" Jasper stood and stretched, appearing disinterested in the findings.

"I got ejected out of his thoughts before I could

ask more questions." I swung my feet over the edge of the bed, and pins and needles erupted in my numb limbs. I rubbed at my legs to regain sensation. "I need to get more information."

Jasper swatted at me. One benefit from temporarily losing the feeling in my legs was not feeling his claws pierce the material of my leggings, but the new snag he left confirmed they had.

"I don't see how you're going to get more information from Mulder," Jasper said. "You don't know how you got into his thoughts just now. You could end up anywhere the next time. Plus, you don't know how or why the spell ended. If you tried again with that voodoo magic, you might end up stuck there. I wouldn't press your luck."

Even though he didn't seem too keen on me teaming up with Mulder, his arguments were valid. "Then I'll have to do it another way. I need to find out how Aunt Mid died and determine if there really was a murder."

I found Grace sitting in what used to be Aunt Mid's office, looking through a stack of papers. Closer inspection revealed they were bills. Most of them had the word OVERDUE stamped on them in big, red letters.

I sat in the chair facing Grace and noted her

pained expression, causing me to hold my initial questions about her aunt. "What's wrong?"

She sighed and leaned back in her chair. "I don't know where to start. There are so many bills past due. I'm not sure how I'm going to pay them. I can't believe Aunt Mid would let things get this bad."

"The fate of the inn might have been out of her hands. She listed it for sale a few months ago." Grace frowned while studying a document. "Then she pulled the listing two weeks before she died according to this."

She lifted a stack of bills and let them flutter to the desktop. "Who would buy this place in its current condition? Whether I decide to sell it or keep it, I need money to pay these off."

That much was true. The inn looked like it was falling down where it stood.

"Janice came by today," Grace said with a sigh.

"What? Did she have more beauty products?"

Grace waved me off. "She's just being nice. She said there might be an interested buyer if I want to sell. But they might tear it down and build something more modern." Grace sighed. "She didn't have to share that information with me. I got the impression that she feels bad about the state of the inn and is trying to give me options."

"Do you think Belinda is the interested buyer?" I asked.

"I don't know. Why would she want to tear it down?" She shrugged. "Maybe selling it would be for the best."

Seeing Grace appear so crestfallen broke my heart. "What were you leaning toward? If you could disregard the bills and the appearance, what would you do if the circumstances were ideal?"

Grace turned toward the glass double doors leading to the small adjoining balcony overlooking the grounds. I followed her gaze—a dusting of snow had fallen. In the dusky hours, the lights on the surrounding pine trees were twinkling against the snowflakes. It was beautiful. That thought coming from someone like me, who never put much stock into the holidays, was saying something.

"I remember Aunt Mid working in the office. I used to ask her why she had an office with a balcony on the second floor if she was afraid of heights." Grace smiled. "She said she liked to challenge herself to face her fears. But as far as I know, that's all she did—face the balcony. She never went out on it. I think she liked to be in the thick of things. With the ballroom next door and the adjoining balcony, she was never far from the fun." She paused and then said, "If everything was ideal? I'd keep it."

Her expression was wistful. "On the drive here, I thought about the times I visited when I was young. It was magical. I mean, like magic without needing the talents of a witch. Every day was like waking up on Christmas morning. I know the viewpoint of a child warped some of those memories, but when we arrived this morning, it brought that all back and I just felt ... content."

I slapped my hand on the desk, pushing the bills aside. "Then it's decided. You keep it."

6

"What?" Grace's eyed widened. "Have you looked around? We're light years away from ideal circumstances. I almost wish I hadn't come back to see how far Kringle Inn has fallen from my memories. I would've rather continued to remember it how it used to be," she said with a look of resignation.

"Then we bring it back to how it used to be." I said the words with more enthusiasm than I felt; I couldn't bear seeing my friend so distraught. "We're witches. There's nothing out of our reach."

Grace laughed and ran a hand through her hair, twisting a red coil around her finger. "That's why we are cocktail servers."

"There's nothing wrong with that." I paced in front of the desk as I made my point. "You're wonderful at whatever you do. We both are. I chose my profession, but this inn chose you. You're good with people."

She twisted her lips to the side and studied her hands. "I suppose so."

"I know so." It felt weird to be the one giving the pep talk; usually that was Grace's department. I looked around the heavily decorated room. "It's time to get back to the basics. Let's think this through. Why does this place have a Christmas theme? How did the inn make money the rest of the year?"

Grace tapped her fingers on her chin, contemplating. "From what I remember, and from the rambling stories Arthur can't stop sharing with me, Christmastime was the biggest money-making season, of course. Outside in the garden, there would be caroling stations for hot chocolate and craft tables. Then they'd hold a holiday ball. There was a Christmas-themed dance each month, all year long. Because who doesn't want to keep the magic of Christmas alive?" The slight smile tugging at the corner of Grace's lips dissolved when she looked around. "But this place doesn't inspire holiday memories. More like the need to start de-hoarding and cleaning. There's no way to get this all done."

"I'll help."

We both turned to the door and saw Nick standing there.

He shrugged, the heat of a blush climbing his neck. "I'll be glad to help, and I'm sure others would, too."

Grace gaped at him. "Why would you want to? I'm not sure if I can pay you much of anything, with all the overdue bills Aunt Mid left."

Nick strode into the room. "Overdue bills?" He frowned. "Hard to believe. Mid was always efficient about staying on top of her debts. But regardless, I'd be happy to bring the holiday spirit back into this place and restore it to the vigor I remember when I was young. The town needs that."

After a minute of uncomfortable silence, Nick cleared his throat. "Well, the offer is there. I have work to do."

I scowled at Nick's retreating form and then lowered my voice, whispering, "Why is he still here? Do you think he's poking around to cause more trouble for me?"

"Marissa, it's not always about you. I think he's a nice guy who cares about the inn." Grace turned to me, her never-ending optimism returning. "I guess it wouldn't hurt to see what we can do. How far did you get with the decorations?"

"Um, well, about that..." I turned to ensure Nick

had left the room and wouldn't do another pop-in. Who knew what other prying ears were around? There was no simple way to explain how I'd cast a voodoo-like spell and inadvertently ended up in Mulder's thoughts, or that he told me about Mid's murder. "I was kind of busy."

"Surely, you'll put your personal dislike of Christmas aside to help me out? I'll put you in charge of the ball. It will be like you're working at the club. You've helped organize those kinds of things before, right? Glenda can help you," Grace said.

"Glenda?" She was the last person I'd consider helpful. "You're joking, right? She's more of a grinch than me. Heck, she rivals the Wicked Witch of the West."

Grace stood. "Then you two can exchange spells. Thanks again for coming with me." She pulled me into a quick hug. She was wearing a thick sweater to shield the cold drafts prevalent in the old architecture of the inn, and she could barely get her arms around me.

First, I needed to find out how Aunt Mid had died. Glenda might not be forthcoming with any information. Being helpful didn't fit her style, but I also didn't want to press the issue with Grace. She had enough to worry about without me questioning her again about whether her aunt's death was a murder.

"No problem," I said. My friend was a hugger, but her embrace still took me by surprise since I was dwelling on the unsavory prospect of working with Glenda. Although, from the way Grace had described her Aunt Mid, she was as cheerful as her niece. Sometimes, an overabundance of their overly optimistic personality could wear you to the core. Perhaps Glenda snapped after one Christmas song too many during the summer months?

❧

FOR AN INN THAT WASN'T EVEN LARGE, I COULDN'T find Glenda anywhere the next day.

One benefit of having to search for her was that I gave myself a self-guided tour. Despite the structure's obvious age and state of disrepair, it also had something more. It had charm.

I'd told Grace to go with her instincts and keep the inn, if that was what she wanted. But even if we held the Christmas ball, it did not convince me we could save the place.

Now, after wandering through all the nooks and crannies of the building, I thought there might've been a chance.

I was no architect, but even I could identify the fine woodwork and beautiful moldings in each room. Many had their own individual holiday theme and were identified as such with a placard outside the room. Whether it was a certain color scheme or a holiday tradition, it made me want to keep going from one room to another for the next discovery.

I also learned more about Christmas than I'd ever desired. The décor told stories about the Christmas star, Saint Nicholas, and traditions of creating gingerbread houses. It presented the history of ornaments by comparing their changes over the centuries. Not to mention enough nutcracker displays to make me uncomfortable of them possibly coming to life while I slept.

I made a mental note to ask Grace to never put me in the Nutcracker Room.

While gazing at the molding around the entrance to the ballroom, Sabina almost smacked me with the door as she exited.

"Oh, sorry. I didn't see you," Sabina glanced at me, and then her gaze slid away.

I opened my mouth, but before I could get a word out, I coughed on the cloying fragrance surrounding Sabina.

"I have chores to do. I must go," she said, hurrying down the hall. Perhaps she thought it was better to flee in case I planned to ask her for another spell.

After a few moments of coughing and gasping, I caught my breath. “Someone needs to tell her that a little perfume goes a long way,” I said to myself.

When I entered the ballroom—which was the largest room in the inn—I found it empty except for Sparkles and Sabina’s lingering scent. The calico took one look at me and made a beeline out of there. I'd found the one cat that didn't care for me.

I crossed my arms and gave the ballroom a once over. It was nothing like the club where I worked, but it had potential. One area offered the perfect spot for a dance floor. Holiday decorations might not have been my thing, but cocktails and dancing were my specialty. Perhaps I could pull this ball off after all.

As I scanned the room, my gaze stopped on the large glass double doors leading to the balcony that oversaw the grounds. I spotted Glenda.

“Finally.” I crossed the floor and went out to the balcony, quickly closing the door behind me to keep the cold from rushing into the old building. “What in the goddess are you doing out here? It's freezing.”

Glenda took a drag on her cigarette and exhaled a cloud of smoke. She turned to me and pressed out the cigarette on the railing.

“It's my break. Now give me a break.” She pushed

past me into the ballroom. “Where's Sparkles? Did you scare her off? You're as bad as that dog of yours.”

“I don't think they permit smoking in the inn,” I said, stumbling over the doorframe in my haste to follow her.

Glenda narrowed her eyes. “Who are you to say? I've been working here for ages. You? You just arrived. Currently, there *is* no boss.”

“Grace is your boss,” I said, because I thought she would be. As long as the bill collectors didn't show up and demand restitution.

“She can tell me not to smoke, then.” Glenda cocked a hand on her hip in a challenge.

I was certain Grace wouldn't permit smoking. Witches had an enhanced sense of smell. The unpleasant scent of smoke would linger long after the cigarette. Most witches never smoked for that reason, not if they wanted to stir an effective spell. Much of choosing the proper ingredients depended on a sense of smell, and smoking reduced it.

But this wasn't the time to argue, even if I felt I could easily take out this cranky scarecrow. Glenda was all sharp angles and bony protrusions. Her scalp was bursting with bristly straw-like hair. Vanity obviously wasn’t one of her faults.

I needed information and her help. I'd start with the less abrasive topic. “Grace wants to restore the inn to its former glory, or at least revive some of the old festivities. One thing she'd like for me to work on, with your help, is the holiday ball."

"The holiday ball? They haven't had that here for years," Glenda said as her gaze grew wistful. "Ernie and I used to tear up the dance floor." She smiled, but only briefly. "He was my husband. He died a long time ago."

I found it hard to envision Glenda doing any type of dancing, but perhaps when Ernie died, something had died within her, as well. "Why did they stop holding it? Did people quit coming?"

"No. Most people around here eat that stuff up. Especially the non-magical. But that's because Mid put so much of herself, and her magic, into making the ball so extraordinary. She was a powerful witch, but it got to be too much for her," Glenda said.

My eyes widened. Glenda wasn't a witch. At least I hadn't detected that scent on her. But she didn't quite smell mortal, either.

"Don't give me that look. I knew she was a witch. I have a little magic blood in me, but not enough to do anything with it. Believe me, I've tried." She snapped her mouth shut and looked away. "Having magic blood has extended my life span, but what's the point when I have to spend years and years alone?"

"I'm sorry." Witches did live longer, which could be a cruel joke if you cared for mortals and outlived those you loved.

Glenda ran her gaze over me and then raised a brow. "Why are you asking about the ball? Do you think you have enough magic in you to recreate that? Doesn't look like it, from where I'm standing."

I clenched my hands in frustration. Glenda had quickly changed my sympathy to aggravation. I inhaled a deep breath to temper my frustration, reminding myself that her anger may have grown from years of loneliness. If we were going to pull this off, I needed her on my side. "I might. Don't worry about that. We'll get it taken care of. Give me the details of what the ball involved."

"It involved a lot of magic to make it happen." Glenda twisted her lips as if she'd soured at the thought. "If you ask me, there's too much emphasis on magic. Our town relies on the income from mortals to keep it going. The paranormals here like to show off. Frankly, I think that's why Mid did it. She tempered her magic all year and then let it all hang out at the holidays."

She shook her head. "Her excessively cheerful attitude was annoying most of the year, but at Christmastime...it was enough to make you want to kill her."

Someone sounded jealous. Surely this wasn't Glenda's bizarre manner of confessing? "What happened to Mid?"

"She died." Glenda circled around the bar we'd been standing next to and wiped off the counter.

I rolled my eyes. "Obviously, I know that. I mean, how did she die?"

"She stopped breathing. Her heart stopped beating. Isn't that what usually happens? Magical people think they can live forever, but even witches die sometimes." She lowered her gaze to study her reflection on the bar top.

The vehemence in her words took me aback, but I wanted to push her—to validate Mulder's belief that Aunt Mid was murdered. Glenda's comment had made me consider Aunt Mid's magic blood. She had been old, but not that old for a witch. "What killed her?"

Glenda shrugged. "Most likely the broken neck she got when she fell from the balcony."

"Which balcony?" Until now, I'd assumed, as Grace did, that an ailment had caused her demise.

Glenda pointed to the double doors behind us. "That one."

I frowned and settled onto a barstool. "You mean the one where you like to sneak out and smoke?"

"I have a lot of places I go to smoke, not just this

balcony," Glenda said with a glare. "Besides, the balcony extends along the front of the building by Mid's office."

"Smoking isn't healthy for you."

"Why? Because it will shorten my never-ending life span? Perhaps that's the plan." Glenda quieted, and her anger deflated, leaving her looking sad. "Ernie's been gone for so long. There are so many memories here. I thought staying would help me stay close to him, but sometimes it seems like as long as this place is standing it's a constant unhappy reminder of what I've lost. Mid was the only one left here who knew me then. Who knew Ernie. Now that she's gone, there's no one but me left to keep his memory alive."

"I'm very sorry about Ernie and all my questions. Mid had fallen? I didn't realize." I didn't add—*to her death*. That made two deadly falls at the inn. It sure sounded suspicious to me.

"It was a surprise to most of us. She never went out on the balcony. That's why it was the best place for me to smoke. Mid was afraid the whole thing would collapse." Glenda smiled. "That never bothered me. I've been tempting death for years, but it doesn't seem to want me."

It surprised me that Mid had been out there at all. She wasn't only afraid of it collapsing; she was also afraid of heights. I almost said as much, but kept my suspicions to myself. Glenda's reported friendship with Mid now made her an unlikely candidate, but she was reckless and a jealous witch. That combination left room for "accidents".

Glenda pursed her lips and her chin wobbled. I was better with animals than people, but even I could tell that she needed a friend, or at least a kind word. I wasn't great at either, but there was one thing I could offer.

"You know what you need?" When Glenda narrowed her eyes with suspicion, I was quick to add, "What we both need? A cocktail. I may not be good at a lot of things, but I make the best charmed cocktails."

Glenda glanced at the liquor bottles lining the shelves behind her. Most were thick with dust except for a select few that were probably Belinda's preference, or those of the few infrequent guests. "I don't know..."

I waved her off. "Come on around here and have a seat. Enter my office. The bar is really my element, you know. Well, maybe you don't know, but you're about to find out."

⁂ 7 ⁂

I circled around the bar. *Where did Mid keep her potion ingredients?* While walking through the inn, I hadn't seen a sign of any. Even if she'd not been active with spelling or potions for a while, I didn't know any witch who didn't keep at least a few ingredients on hand.

The bar seemed like the most likely place, since it had a refrigerator and a small burner for heating coffee—or potion ingredients. Mid might've had a room in the attic, or if she feared someone might find her magic stash, somewhere less accessible. But considering her fear of heights, I found that less likely. From the appearance of the abandoned bar, it didn't seem like anyone would bother anything here, anyway.

"Let's see what we have here." I bent to peer under the bar.

"Aha!" Extra napkins, drink stirrers, and a stack of envelopes concealed a few vials and bottles. I recognized the peeling labels and vague scent of magic surrounding them and pulled the potion ingredients out to hold them up in victory.

Glenda eyed the vials warily. She wasn't impressed. "Do you think you should use those? Who knows how long that stuff has been there. Or even what it is."

"They're fine. Potions don't expire." Well, some did, but this wasn't the time to point that out. Or to dwell on a prior situation when an expired or incorrect ingredient may have contributed to a death—although I hadn't been the one using the stuff, only the one solving the case.

I set out a few glasses. "Didn't you say that you loved to tempt death?"

"I didn't realize you were going to hold me to it," Glenda said with a frown.

"What's your concern with a little old potion? No one has died from my charmed cocktails ... yet." My wink didn't ease her wary expression.

Making cocktails gave me a chance to search through the potion ingredients. The only ones who probably had any reason to use this event hall were

Glenda, as the event coordinator, or Sabina, the housekeeper. Either would have had access to the ingredients and enough knowledge to make them dangerous if they wanted to stir something up to get rid of Mid. Some mixtures were difficult to detect in a drink but could cause indigestion or vomiting. Perhaps they'd added a potion to Mid's drink, and then she'd staggered and fallen from the balcony.

Based on Glenda's confused expression while I mixed ingredients, she either knew little about potions or was a talented actor. I took the test a little further and held up a vial. It was easy to identify as mood magic from the bright purple color, but I feigned ignorance. "What's this?"

"How in the heck am I supposed to know? I told you I know nothing about spells or potions. Are you trying to rub it in?" Glenda scowled and smoothed her hair, which sprang back to attention once she lowered her hand.

"No, I couldn't remember what it was. Oh, yes." After opening the vial and taking a whiff, I nodded. As if experiencing an epiphany, I widened my eyes to see if Glenda would call me on it—this ingredient was odorless. "It's mood magic."

"I don't need any lessons on potions." Glenda spun on her stool and lowered one foot to the floor.

"Wait." I touched her arm and Glenda jerked it

away. "Aren't you going to have a cocktail with me? It will get us in the holiday spirit to plan the ball."

"Fine." She turned her stool back to face me. "As long as you have one, too. If I'm going down, you're going with me. What are you going to make?"

I thought for a moment. "At the club back home, I make a fabulous highball. But we're going to need something new, created for the Kringle Inn. I'll think about what our drink will be. Maybe something with champagne, to celebrate reviving the inn. How about a twist on a mimosa? Those are always fun. We can offer this drink as the special at the ball. We'll call it a holiday highball." I smiled. "Get it? For the ball?"

"Oh, she's funny too." Glenda rolled her eyes and barked out a laugh.

I set out two tall glasses and began preparing the cocktail. "Let's have one. It's a hit with my regulars. A highball originated from drinking whiskey and having a ball. The word high came from serving it in a tall glass. You can choose a different liquor if you prefer, and then I'll add the nonalcoholic mixer and the charmed ingredients."

"I guess you've proved you know your booze. Go ahead, you can pick the liquor and surprise me." Glenda waved her hand. "I can't say I have a preference. I don't even remember the last time I had a drink."

Most paranormals had a high tolerance for liquor, but Glenda claimed to have little, or weak, magic within her blood. I didn't want to make something too strong, so I kept the liquor content minimal. I mixed the potions, including the mood magic, since she could obviously use some cheering up, and it made the drink a bright purple color. Then I garnished the glasses with a wedge of lime on the sides.

I held my glass up. "Cheers to a fabulous holiday ball and bringing the Kringle Inn back to its prime."

Glenda lifted her glass and clinked it with mine. "Sure. As long as your cocktail concoction doesn't kill me first. If it does, I'll see Ernie sooner rather than later."

I lifted the glass to my lips and hesitated. I wasn't positive about what some of these vials might contain and had taken my best guess. If I was going to make cocktails for the party, I'd need to stock up on fresh ingredients.

Glenda took a big swallow and smacked her lips. "This isn't bad."

I took a sip. Darn, I was a good mixologist. I'd admit I've had some fails, though the results were rarely worse than indigestion. Hopefully, the ingredients for treating that were here if we needed them, or Glenda would never forgive me.

As EXPECTED, BOTH MEMBERS OF MY FUR FAMILY were hiding out in my room. Mulder was playing with something on the floor, and I found Jasper lounging on the window seat.

He turned to me when I plopped down beside him. "I need to run some things by you."

"It's about time that you came for my guidance," Jasper said.

I smiled. "After one of my specialty highballs this afternoon, Glenda was more amicable. She seems to get friendlier once she loosens up."

"Whatever. Let's hear your great deductions and how you determined the most likely suspects, all while planning the Christmas ball and having cocktails." Jasper twitched his tail. "I think it's the highball talking."

"You're just jealous because I'm doing all the sleuthing while you've been lying around. Now, back to Glenda and her potential for being responsible for Mid's death. Besides hating Mid's optimistic attitude, and someone who likes to sneak out for a smoke on the balcony in question, she was jealous of Aunt Mid's magic. Jealousy can be a nasty thing and drive people to do things they don't normally do."

Jasper rolled on his back, giving me an eyeful.

"You could show a little modesty," I suggested.

Jasper shimmied around on his back to gain enough momentum to flop onto his side. "There, is that better for your innocent eyes? I can't imagine that I could offend you. I've seen the skimpy outfits people wear in the night club. It's disgusting. Someone needs to tell them to cover up. Without fur, that plucked-looking flesh is just ..." Jasper shuddered. "Repulsive, I tell you. I don't know how you can look at yourself in the mirror after you shower."

"Enough. I've heard your complaints before, but while we're talking about what's disgusting, remember that I'm the one who cleans up your hairballs. That takes disgusting to a whole other level."

"I can't help that. I have to keep myself clean. It's my nature. The clothes humans choose to wear is their choice." He stuck his nose in the air.

I sighed and dropped the subject. Jasper never liked to lose an argument, or end without getting the last word.

Mulder lay on the rug at the foot of the bed and perked his head up from where he'd been resting it on his paws, revealing what he'd concealed there.

"Where did you get that?" I grabbed the tiny cat voodoo doll and pocketed it.

Mulder's tongue lolled out as he panted and cocked his head from side to side. His oblivious nature made me wonder if I might have imagined our conversation during the spell. I wished I could've stayed in his head long enough to get more information about Aunt Mid's murder.

Jasper gasped at the tiny replica. "Why do you still have that? And you let him get it? For goddess' sake, witch! Who knows what could happen if that cat doll got in the wrong hands? Find out how to get rid of that properly, risking no unexpected repercussions."

"What if I want to try the spell again with you some day? Besides, it's cute." I waggled the little cat figure back and forth. "It even has the little white spot under your chin."

"Don't even think about it. I don't need you in my head. Besides, that thing looks nothing like me. It's an insult. Why not go make a replica of that tub of fur on the floor? It would be a lot easier. Get a pair of googly eyes and stick them on a round pom-pom, and there you go." Jasper settled on the cushion and smiled at the image he'd provided.

"Okay, enough picking on your brother." He and Mulder still had a tenuous relationship. I'd hoped this trip would be a chance for them to become more like friends than tolerant enemies.

"My what? I told you he's not my brother. We

look nothing alike. Our fur is not even the same color, and he's a dog, for catnip's sake!"

Both of them being stubborn males and of two different species didn't help them grow the love. "You were both adopted, so technically, that makes you brothers. You don't have to look the same to be part of the same family."

The expression of horror on Jasper's face was worth bringing it up again. He liked me reminding him he was part of our family, but he preferred I neglect to include Mulder in that unit.

I crossed my legs under me. "I need to talk through the potential suspects for Aunt Mid's murder."

Jasper relaxed with the change of subject. "I thought you were supposed to be working on Christmas decorations."

I waved him off. "I'll get to that. It shouldn't be too hard with a little magic."

Mulder paused in his panting, and Jasper's eyes widened. "Great. So, you're going to blow up or burn the place down? I hope Grace has insurance."

"You have no faith in me. It's decorations. How hard of a spell can that be? It was mostly mortals that used to come to the ball. I can use a glamour spell if needed."

Neither needed to say a word to remind me of the

trouble I'd had with spells before. Jasper and Mulder both stared at me, wide-eyed. Since Mulder had said that he saw spirits, I wondered if it wasn't just me he was looking at. A spirit could stand right behind me, and I wouldn't know it.

"I've improved significantly. You both know that. I'm making a new specialty cocktail for the ball. I found some of Mid's old potions ..."

"Old potions!" Jasper shrieked. "You have enough trouble with new ingredients, and now you're going to mess around with old potions? They may not even have the components you think are in them. Who knows how long Mid had them sitting around?"

"I'll get new ingredients. You worry too much. I want to talk about Mid now. We'll worry about the cocktails later." I ignored the stirring of unease in my stomach that validated everything he said.

Jasper stared at me for a long beat. "You better hope Christmas miracles are possible, or you might help to hasten the end of the inn for Grace. Then she won't have to decide."

I ignored his lack of confidence and changed the subject. The arguments we've had about my charmed cocktails went on forever. Neither of us would back down, and I'd remind him that one of my cocktails going haywire resulted in him being able to talk to me. He would retort that another misspelling could end our connection—or remind me of how I blew up the bathroom wall at Night Moves.

"Here's what I'm thinking so far. I agree with Mulder that it was a murder. Aunt Mid was afraid of heights. What would get her out on that balcony? Glenda is our most likely suspect." I held up my hand to silence Jasper. "I know she claims they were friends, but hear me out. We can't rule her out just because of her claim. No one else has mentioned them being besties. Even if they were, sometimes relationships can take a drastic turn if emotions are running high and end with hating those you used to love."

Jasper climbed to a pillow that was sitting in a patch of sunlight to curl up. He said, "I find it hard to believe that Glenda could be besties with anyone."

"Or she could be the interested buyer. Maybe she wants to tear the inn down to get rid of old, painful memories," I said. "Once Mid decided she wasn't going to sell, Glenda might've killed her in the hopes of getting rid of the inn with her."

Mulder's gaze volleyed from me to Jasper as he tried to follow the conversation. Or I simply fascinated him with the way I tossed my hands around when I talked. Each time I rested my hand on the bed, he sniffed it to ensure I wasn't concealing a treat.

Agreeing with his assumption about Aunt Mid's

murder seemed to please him. If I was interpreting his minor change in expression correctly, at least.

He craned to lick my palm and then retreated with a whine after determining that I didn't have anything. Perhaps I didn't understand him at all.

"The next suspect would be Belinda. She's practically made the inn her home away from home. Maybe she couldn't stand the current state of the inn. Or she wanted to buy it for herself." I thought for a moment. "Sabina told me that Mid was thinking of telling Belinda she couldn't bring Wilber to stay anymore. Did you see the damage he did to the woodwork around the fireplace in the library? He started with the extra logs and almost chewed his way through the wall."

"That's it? That's your extensive list of suspects?" Jasper rolled back onto his side. "You can't come up with more than that?"

"Well, there only needs to be one murderer. We don't need a huge list," I said.

"What about Sabina, the maid? She and Glenda would've had access to those potions," he said. "Or the realtor, Janice? Maybe she wanted to sell it for the commission."

I nodded. "I thought of that." It was odd how our thoughts were on the same track. Maybe his destiny was to be my familiar.

"Besides, Sabina's into that Cajun voodoo, hocus pocus, or shrinking heads stuff." Jasper's gaze strayed to my pocket, where I'd stored his tiny fabric doppelgänger. "Something could've gone amiss. It might've been an accidental murder. Remember what happened when you tried that spell. We all know you've had multiple magical mishaps. We're lucky it hasn't resulted in someone's death, yet."

"Maybe. She almost ran into me hurrying from the ball room today." I shook my head. "But I don't think it's her. She freaked out when she saw Steve. She doesn't seem to have the stomach for murder, or the desire to work with voodoo. I had to pressure her a little to convince her to give me the spell," I said.

She might've given me the spell, so I'd leave her alone. Or was Jasper right when he said she might have known about my spelling inadequacies? Had she hoped I might have an unfortunate accident so I'd stop asking questions about Mid?

8

We were getting nowhere fast with our hodgepodge investigation. I felt like I was going in more circles than Jasper completed before settling for a nap.

Jasper wiggled his whiskers and said, "How about the rest of the staff? I suspect the elves. More are arriving today to help with the decorating."

"We don't know that they're elves," I said, suppressing the flicker of hope surging within me. What if it was true? If the dreams about the magic of Christmas squelched in my childhood were real?

"Whatever," Jasper said with the exasperated tone of a teenager. "Arthur said they're cheap labor infatuated with Christmas, but they creep me out. One of them tried to put a Santa hat on me. When I backed away, he came at me with one of those headbands with the reindeer antlers. Forcing me to wear either of those is a crime."

I pressed my lips together to avoid smiling at the image. "I doubt anyone here would agree that looking cute or getting into the holiday spirit is a crime. Creeping you out isn't a sufficient motive for murder."

Jasper sniffed. "What you need is a better plan... or any plan. What about that police officer? Does he have any leads? Besides you, of course."

"I don't know. I've avoided him since his suggestion that I might kill someone who looked like an elf because I don't care for Christmas." Granted, the overabundance of holiday decor put me in a foul mood, but not enough to kill someone.

"I'll go talk to Nick. At least then I can be sure he's ruled me out as a suspect." I stood, eager to leave now that I'd decided. A trip into town sounded promising. It might've been helpful to get away from here for a while.

"This conversation has exhausted me. I've barely gotten in my six hours a day of napping since we've been here," Jasper said, settling on the window seat. "Hurry back."

"Don't worry about me. I'll be fine," I said with sarcasm at his lack of concern.

Mulder scrambled to his feet to follow me. "Sorry, buddy. I think you'd better wait here." Most likely, the police station or any stores I might've needed to visit wouldn't permit him inside. Plus, if I was walking into town, it would take forever to get there with him. He had to stop and sniff every two seconds.

I felt bad leaving him, especially now that I knew how intelligent he might've been. I reached to pat his head. "You keep an eye out and watch after Grace, little guy." He continued to pant and wag his tail, leaving me to wonder what was going on in his mind behind those big, bulbous eyes.

THE EVENING WALK TO THE POLICE STATION WAS longer than I expected with my limited exercise regime. However, it gave me a chance to see the rest of the area. I hadn't realized we were that isolated from town, but getting lost on my way back would be a challenge. The thick variety of pine, fir, and spruce trees surrounding the inn had signs hanging from giant plastic candy canes and nestled in Christmas displays, pointing the way to the Kringle Inn. It was like I was emerging from Santa's village at the North Pole.

They strung the trees along the way with lights,

although many were out. The woods and the beauty of nature reminded me of what I loved about my home state of Pennsylvania. If Grace stayed, I'd have another reason to return to visit.

I arrived at the quaint little village of Tinsel Town. When we'd driven through, I had paid little attention. The town square had a huge, decorated Christmas tree. The brightly colored decor of the buildings surrounding it resembled the children's game about a land made of candy or life-sized gingerbread houses. Although obnoxiously overdone, somehow it didn't come across as corny. Instead, it was warm and comforting.

What was happening to me? Was I falling under the holiday spell?

Each person I passed smiled and waved and wished me happy holidays or season's greetings. It almost had me wondering if something was in the peppermint hot chocolate prominently advertised on the window of the coffee shop. One way to find out...

In the café, I ordered the specialty and discovered it was delicious. As it warmed my belly, I continued my walk through town. The atmosphere was strangely hypnotic, and I felt my holiday disdain dissolving. Or was there really something in the hot chocolate?

I paused at the storefront displays filled with toys,

model trains, and other trinkets that would inspire most children to add them to their lists and have adults reminisce about the holidays of their youth. Each business had a holiday wreath on the door and a streetlamp painted like a candy cane.

The Christmas music that piped through the town filled me with holiday cheer, despite a lifelong resistance. So much so that I popped into a store called "Christmas for Every Day" and picked up a few ugly sweaters, Santa caps, a white fake fur-lined skirt, and tights with a candy cane pattern.

I hadn't decided if I'd end up being brainwashed enough to wear any of these holiday items, or if I would give them as revenge gifts for those who'd mocked my avoidance of what I called Christmas consumerism.

To be sure I left no one out, I picked up matching pet sweaters and caps at the Christmas Critters store. I even got one for Wilber, although I had my doubts it would fit.

The police station was in the center of town. I made a beeline for the door when a few carolers spotted me and began heading my way. If my weird mood continued, there was a risk that I'd join them and burst into song. I rushed into the station and closed the door behind me, leaning on it as if I were running from the devil himself rather than some hopped-up Christmas carolers.

The front desk was empty, so I rang the bell on the counter, relieved that it let out a normal jangle instead of blaring out a holiday tune. Gaudy garland surrounded the reception desk.

Nick emerged from the back, looking none too pleased to see me. "If the Grinch herself hasn't arrived at our little version of Whoville."

"Hilarious. I'd hate to see what you do for the other holidays the rest of the year," I said with a nod toward the door and the overabundance of Christmas decor I'd barely escaped. When my head bumped against something, I looked up. They'd tied a bright red bow to a chunk of mistletoe to hang above the door. "Really? Mistletoe at a police station?"

Nick's smile brought a twinkle to his eyes. "Why not?"

I rolled my eyes and stepped away from the dangling plant. "Now I've seen everything."

He shook his head. "No, you haven't, and be glad of that. The decorations here are courtesy of the receptionist, Marge. She stepped out for her break," he said, regarding the station lobby with dismay. "She toned this down. You should see the break room."

I laughed at the misery that briefly clouded his

expression. "You're saying that even you tire of Christmas?"

"It's not Christmas the entire year for the town, just for the Kringle Inn. We enjoy some of the other holidays, although there are those who have enough Christmas holiday spirit to keep it alive all year long, and why not? What harm does it do to be more friendly, more giving, and to smile at a stranger?" Nick gestured that I should follow and turned to walk into his office. He settled into a chair behind his desk, leaving the door open to provide a view of the front area.

"I guess when you put it that way."

I wouldn't admit it to him, but the atmosphere of the town had improved my mood. That is, until I feared it might tempt me to join the carolers. That wouldn't have been good for anyone. My dancing skills were spectacular—not my singing.

I followed him into his office but stayed standing. Sitting in the chair facing him felt too much like I was being questioned. "I'm assuming you've finished your investigation and I'm off the hook for Steve?"

He waved me off and shuffled through some paperwork on his desk. "We ruled his death accidental."

"That's what Mulder thought."

I clamped my mouth shut. How would I explain

my dog had told me he could tell that Steve's death was an accident by the lingering scent? That he claimed he could detect the victim's scent prior to death and determine whether it was terror or fear? That he could see ghosts of the recently deceased to determine if the cause of death was intentional or accidental?

Nope, not a conversation to start with a mortal, even if he believed in magic. The magic of Christmas, at least.

"Mulder, who's that?" Nick glanced up from the paperwork and drew his brows down.

"Oh, that's my dog. I meant to say one of the other workers told me it was an accident. I'm not sure about his name. There have been so many new people to meet."

My laugh felt forced, and Nick's pointed look confirmed it wasn't all that convincing. "But I'm glad you agree that I'm guilty of nothing more than not caring for Christmas."

"This is your chance to discover the magic of the holiday. You might change your mind after your visit. The Christmas spirit grows on you, especially if you're at the Kringle Inn. It's a Christmas oasis for people who can't get enough of that holiday." His smile was wistful. "I used to go there every year as a kid. We'd stay there during their big Christmas in

July event to enjoy a little of that wonder midyear. Nothing like it."

"Speaking of the inn, I was wondering what your thoughts were about Aunt Mid's death?"

"You mean Grace's Aunt Mid?" He pushed his chair back so he could cross his ankle over his knee. "Are you related to Grace?"

"No, but we're very close friends," I said. I might've needed a little charm without using magic to get him to talk since there were sure to be confidentiality rules. "Listen, Grace is overwhelmed. I heard her aunt died from a fall from a balcony, and also that height terrified her. Something doesn't add up. Why would she be on the balcony?"

I couldn't add that my concern was because of my dog telling me her death wasn't accidental.

He nodded. "I've thought about that, but with no eyewitness to provide any proof, we're ruling it as accidental. We have no way to prove anything differently, unless someone comes forward and confesses to murdering her. That's not likely to happen."

"What if you had someone on the inside? Kind of like an assistant on the case?" I perched on the edge of his desk until he looked pointedly at my behind and its inappropriate placement. I slid off and lowered myself into the chair facing the desk.

"The inside of what?" Nick leaned back in his

chair and folded his arms. His skeptical expression implied he knew exactly what I was referring to. "Besides, there is no case."

"Let's say there was one. If there's a possibility of the involvement of foul play, you'd want to examine every option." If only I had one of my charmed cocktails to offer him, or if I could mutter a spell. Then I'd have a better chance of getting him to agree.

"I would. I loved Mid like family. But, as you can see," he motioned around the vacant police station, "I'm understaffed. We don't have a lot of crime in this area, so it's not usually a problem. But we get busier as Christmas nears, and I get a few extra deputies to help."

"Make me an honorary deputy, or investigator, or ... something." I tried on my sweetest smile.

He raised a brow.

Apparently, my smile wasn't sweet enough, or he was immune to my charms. The latter seemed more certain. "Or not. Okay, let me report back to you if I find out anything. It would make me feel like I was helping Grace."

"I thought you were helping with renovations and the holiday ball." He sighed. "Although, I have to admit that doesn't seem like your area of expertise."

"I am helping. But that stuff is nothing. I'm an experienced cocktail waitress and mixologist. I deal with enormous crowds every night. It's definitely in my area of expertise." I might not be great at magic, but a simple glamour or illusion spell should take care of the decorations.

Nick spoke of other areas where I lacked expertise. "You don't have experience working with a case, as you call it."

"I have more experience with that than I do in Christmas decorating."

Having to defend my skills was frustrating. I'd helped solve three cases in Florida—well, Jasper and I had. At least a few people accepted that I might have a knack for this. But those people were also of the paranormal variety, who were ready to accept explanations that weren't always believed by mortals. Like working a case with the help of a cat and a dog.

"Really?" His comment landed heavy with sarcasm.

I nodded, not wanting to go into detail about exactly how I'd helped with those cases. Otherwise, I'd have to discuss Jasper, magic, and potions—all things which Grace had asked me to keep quiet about since she wasn't sure how the people in this town felt about magic.

Usually I didn't give a darn, but Grace might've been here for the long haul. She had enough challenges without me making things more difficult.

Nick and I continued our stare-off. He didn't stand a chance. I'd faced down Mulder on more occasions than I could count. I usually lost, but it had improved my stamina during a stare-off. This time it was for Grace. I wasn't going to back down.

9

Nick dropped his gaze and sighed. "Fine. It's nothing official, but if it makes you feel better, and if you don't bother anyone, I'll let you believe that you're looking into the situation. If nothing else, it will allow you to get to know our town and the people in it a little better. I think in the end you might find that you're infected with the holiday spirit after all."

I smiled. I knew a few spirits I might've needed to talk to, but none had anything to do with Christmas. "Sounds like a deal." I stood.

"Oh, and Marissa?"

"Yes?"

"I might stop at the inn now and then to see how things are going for you and if you've made any progress. By the way, how is Grace?" Nick threw that last thing in as a random comment, but his eyes lit up when he said her name.

"She's doing okay. It's a lot to take in, but she can handle it."

Now I knew the real reason he agreed to let me think I was helping on what he assumed was a nonexistent case: Grace.

"Take a few cookies before you go." Nick reached behind him and brought out a plate of decorated sugar cookies. "I made them myself."

I studied the elaborately decorated cookies, cut into the shapes of Christmas trees, gifts, gingerbread men, and stars. "What, no ghosts or skeletons?"

"I'm a police officer. It might be a small town, but I've had to deal with enough skeletons. Although usually around here, they represent the secrets people hide in their closets," he said. "I have no desire to add more. Just wait. Soon you'll agree that Christmas is a better holiday than Halloween."

"Don't hold your breath." I chose a cookie shaped like a star. It reminded me of the decorations at the club at home. "Thanks. It will go with my hot chocolate." I frowned at my almost empty cup and the bags full of impulse purchases. "Do they put something extra in the hot chocolate?"

Nick smiled and leaned back in his chair. "I suppose they could infuse it with Christmas spirit."

"Sure. That must be it." Mid couldn't be the only powerful witch in town; I wondered who made the brew at the coffee shop and if they'd put a charm in it. Although no harm, no foul. My cocktails made people merrier all year round, regardless of whether they had alcohol in them. Why not do the same with hot chocolate?

"Tell Grace I said hello," Nick called after me.

"Sure thing," I said.

I exited slowly as I ensured the street was clear of carolers, noting a familiar face ducking into the Home Aide Realty storefront. Janice. I thought about paying her a visit, but then saw a better option at Ready Readings. The window display had a cartoon image of an old lady with scarves wrapped around her head and draped over her body. Her hands hovered over a crystal ball. Beneath the image it said, *Get the answer to your question by making an appointment with Madame Ambrosia.*

That had to be Sabina's grandmother or someone from her family tree. The little shop looked so out of place compared to the other stores. This was probably the one shop in town that might've had any of the supplies I'd need to mix cocktails for the ball. It was also the only one not decked to the nines with holiday décor. There was only a small pumpkin and gourd display near the door. Closer inspection revealed a snowman carved into the pumpkin and a Santa cap on the gourd.

The bell on the door jangled when I entered. The room was empty except for a glass countertop display. I peered through the glass to see tarot cards, crystal balls, incense, herbs, and voodoo dolls that looked much better than my half-hearted attempt. Most of what was on display were the trinkets non-magical folk came to expect in a store like this. I wondered if Madame Ambrosia had the better stuff in the back. It would've been nice to restock my supplies.

As I turned to explore the small area further, a mail slot on the wall caught my eye. I'd initially missed it since it was far below my line of sight; they had placed it at eye level for a child. "You've got to be kidding me. This is where kids deliver letters to Santa?"

The beaded curtain rattled, and a woman stepped out from behind it. "Of course," she said. "Santa operates on magic. Wanting to spread peace and goodwill fuels the magic of Christmas. Who better to ensure that the children's letters arrive safely at the North Pole to grant the wishes of good little boys and girls?"

The woman wore a thick knitted Christmas sweater, complete with a large red pom-pom in the middle of the reindeer's nose. The holiday spirit had even infected the one little magical sanctuary where I thought Halloween would still reign as a top holiday.

"*You're* Madame Ambrosia?" My disappointment was evident in my voice. I'd expected the usual over-the-top getup of long flowing gowns, veils—something similar to the cartoon depiction on the window. "Really? A holiday sweater?"

She shrugged. "If you can't beat them, you might as well join them."

I sighed. "It's a sad day when you can't find one spooky item this close to Halloween."

She spread her arms wide. "The holiday is a state of mind. Not what you wear, or how you decorate."

It sounded like a speech she'd delivered more than once. "Okay, whatever. I know it's no use. Madame Ambrosia, I assume?"

"No. I'm her granddaughter, Sofia. What can I do for you? I noticed you taking in our lovely display. Many of these items make wonderful gifts." She smiled and gestured at the display case in a manner similar to that of a game show host.

I raised a brow. "I don't suppose you know how to do an eye spy spell?"

The smile fell from her face. "Why on earth would you want to do that?"

I shrugged. "I have my reasons."

"No, I don't know how, and if I did, I wouldn't

share it with you. Only Madame Ambrosia would know, and I can't imagine that she'd share that information, either. That spell could have disastrous consequences if done incorrectly." She looked me over, stopping for a moment on the black streak in my hair, and then dropped her sales persona. "Grams—Madame Ambrosia, that is—her mind has gotten a little soft. We have had to install magic wards to ensure she doesn't inadvertently spell someone or something."

I took in the small store. "What do you do in this shop besides sell trinkets?"

She smiled as her sales persona returned. "We tell fortunes, or seek to see the future, of course."

I inhaled deeply. She smelled strongly of magic, but not as intense as the scent from the back room, where I assumed her grandmother spent much of her time.

"Really?" I stretched out the word and punctuated it with a raised brow. The witches' ability to sell magic determined much of people's belief. That was where I often fell short. I wasn't good at selling myself *or* my magic.

"Really." She nodded. "Some things are simple to predict, as I'm sure you know. Since this is Tinsel Town, most of our readings are optimistic ones.

People want to hear that everything is going to be all right. Don't you agree?"

"Sure, that's what people want to hear, but that's not always true," I said.

"The truth is all about how you interpret it. If you believe in something enough, you might swing the truth to your favor," she said.

I rolled my eyes, tiring of her sales pitch. Her spiel would never work on most paranormals. She likely did well, though, since most of her customers were probably mortal. "Sure. How about I stock up on spelling supplies; I assume you have those?"

I picked up the Christmas-themed notepad on the counter by the register. After jotting down a list of the most basic spelling ingredients, I handed it to her.

She ran her gaze over the list and then me again. "Of course. However, these things are a little costly."

"Because you sell so much of them, right?" I said. "Listen, I'm doing this for the Kringle Inn. We're going to have a ball, and my job is to make sure the cocktails are the bomb. Not literally the bomb, but enough to knock the Christmas socks off the visitors and help make the event prosperous for my friend Grace. It's a win-win for everyone in town. Perhaps you'd consider offering a discount."

"Fine. Let me see what I have." She went into the

back, and I peered closer at the baubles under the glass.

When she returned with my requested items, I asked, "How do you survive in this town? It seems like all anyone cares about is Christmas."

"Easy. Christmas is about celebrating the past and looking forward to the future." She tilted her head and smiled as she handed me the bill.

"Okay. Thanks." I paid her and gathered my bags, feeling deflated. I hadn't thought I'd walk in here and get the answers I was looking for, but I thought I'd get at least one.

"Aren't you going to ask your question?" Sofia said.

"No, that's fine." She was only going to tell me what I wanted to hear. There was no use asking her if Aunt Mid was murdered and who the murderer was if she was going to share a hearts-and-flowers prediction.

"Yes, she was," Sofia said.

I paused with my hand on the doorknob and turned back. "She was what? I didn't ask you anything."

"You didn't have to. Yes, she was murdered, and you already know who did it." She backed toward the beaded curtain leading to the hall.

I released the door, and the bell jangled. "Wait. Who did it? Who was it?"

Her voice carried from the back room. "I already answered the question you most wanted to know. That should make you happy. The rest is up to you. I only know what you already know."

❧

THE NEXT MORNING, I AWOKE REINVIGORATED TO solve the case. Nick had somewhat confirmed that he felt there might have been foul play, as had Sofia. Now all I had to do was prove it. I'd also came back with what I thought was a fantastic idea for the ball, but so far, Grace wasn't buying it.

"A costume party?" Grace looked up from the papers spread across the desk and raised a brow.

I nodded. "It will be Halloween, so why not?"

"Look around, Marissa." She pointed at the explosion of holiday decor all around the office. "The whole theme is about Christmas."

I leaned on the edge of her desk as my excitement built. "People can dress up like candy canes, elves, or Santa Claus, if they prefer. I bought a pair of candy cane tights if you need to borrow them." I didn't add that I'd noticed many people already wearing those tights every day, and that I thought it was weird.

I moved closer, trying to channel Sofia's saleswoman pitch. "We need something unique. The town loves Christmas, but as you can see, some areas of the inn will not be completely up to par by the time of the party. We can use the current state of disrepair as part of the Halloween theme, while offering something the town has never had before—a Christmas-themed Halloween ball, or call it a dance. Everyone loves to dress up, right?"

Grace rubbed her chin as she contemplated the suggestion. "I don't know. You're thinking like a witch."

"You say that like it's a bad thing. This is a way to pull everyone in from town. They have renovated a lot in town while the inn remains stuck in the last decade, or century. And admit it, it's been like a ghost town since we've been here." I gasped as the idea came to me. "I've got it!"

"Got what?" She laughed at my enthusiasm.

I spread my arms to encompass the room. "The theme can be the ghosts of Christmas past. It could remind people of how important the inn is for the town. That it's an imperative part of this community and helps bring in business for everyone. It will be a Merry Hallow-Christmassy celebration."

"I should've known you'd insert Halloween into this." Grace dropped her hands to rest them on the desk. Her gaze was thoughtful. "The ghosts of Christmas past... The idea is growing on me."

I smiled. "This could help with more than revenue for the inn; it could keep Halloween alive amid a never-ending Christmas. It might also bring the killer to the party. Since I could serve a charmed cocktail—or I should say a killer *confession* cocktail—I might wrap up the case that night. Aunt Mid would get the justice she deserves."

Grace was wavering. I gave her that last nudge. "You said I was in charge of the ball. Why not let me run with it? You have enough to deal with."

She looked down at the papers on the desk. "That's true... Fine, but no confession cocktail. Those can produce confessions of unexpected, and undesirable, information. But now you have the hard part."

I flopped into the chair facing her desk. "What hard part? The decorations won't be that difficult, with a little glamour. I know you said you didn't want to rely on magic, but according to Glenda, that's how Mid pulled off the big party. You won't need to use glamour next year once you finish the renovations."

"No. The hard part will be to convince Glenda it's a good idea," she said.

"Oh." I hadn't thought of that. I assumed since I was in charge that I'd just tell Glenda. I might need a few cocktails to make it a Merry Hallow-Christmassy for all. Although, I had found Glenda's soft spot—cats. She adored Sparkles, and the feeling was mutual.

The cat may have been Aunt Mid's and should've rightfully been Grace's now, but as most of us realized rather quickly, cats pick their owner, not the other way around. For some reason, Sparkles felt that her owner was Glenda.

The cat continued to avoid us and seemed spooked by our presence. You'd think that another cat, a dog, and a few witches wouldn't bother her. She practically lived with a pig. But some cats bonded to witches, while others wanted nothing to do with them. Sparkles seemed to fall into the latter category.

Luckily, I had another cat to use to get on Glenda's good side.

10

"There you are." I found Jasper sneaking around in the kitchen and failing to look innocent while eyeing the counter. I shook my head. "You know that's one way to get our welcome revoked. No counters." I'd occasionally looked the other way when he did it at home since I knew my Gran let him get away with it, but we were guests here.

He scowled when he realized I'd busted him. "But there's nothing good left on the floor. Which I'm not accustomed to eating off of. It might be okay with Mulder to be a furry vacuum cleaner and suck up anything people discard, but I require a dish. Which you forgot to bring, I might add."

"I'll get you something else to use. But now I have

a task for you, which involves you being your adorable self." I opened the refrigerator to search for something to feed him, to soften him up for the job. He was incredibly irritable when he was hungry.

Jasper stalked around the kitchen. "Don't forget I need a proper dish to eat from, and it can't be one of Sparkles'. I'm always cute. As for you... Well, you're going to have to work on being cute and adorable on your own. I can't say I've heard those two words used in connection with your name before."

"Very funny. Listen, I need you to help me get on Glenda's good side," I said. I wanted to have Glenda's help, rather than hindrance, in getting the ball and other events rolling.

I gave up on finding anything suitable in the refrigerator and searched through the cupboard until I found a can of tuna.

"Good luck with that. I don't think Glenda likes anything or anyone," Jasper said, holding his tail high as he paced impatiently while I opened the can.

"She loves Sparkles," I said. Sparkles' love for Glenda made me wonder if the cat would feel the same if she thought Glenda had offed Mid. Why? Who knows, but based on the relationship I had with Jasper, it seemed I knew very little about cats.

Jasper hissed when I mentioned the other cat. "That calico is nothing but a nincompoop. With a name like that, I can't say I blame her, though. And she's afraid of her own shadow. Each time I've tried to approach her, she's off like a rocket."

"Perhaps Glenda loves cats instead of people. We need to convince her that the Halloween ball is a good idea and feel her out about Aunt Mid." Glenda didn't know that I could talk to Jasper. Well, most people didn't. It wasn't like I made it public knowledge. But I'd seen her talking with Sparkles. "I'll broach the topic with Glenda and then duck out. You come in next and listen while she talks out her thoughts with you. Unless you'd like to talk to Wilber."

"I'm not talking to that pig. Last time I saw him, Sabina was chasing him because he ate all the popcorn."

"Popcorn?" I said.

"The popcorn was supposed to be used to make popcorn strings to decorate the new Christmas tree in the lobby." Jasper shook his head. "Fine, I'll be sweet with Glenda. I'm sure she won't be able to resist talking to me because I'm such a good listener."

I hid my smile as I scooped the tuna on a plate. The pig terrified Jasper, more so than Glenda. I knew all along that he would choose the lesser of the two evils.

I set his food on the floor.

"I'll do it. But just so you know, I think it's a stupid plan." Jasper approached the food, dipping his nose to sniff the tuna before gobbling it down.

"What's your rush?"

He lifted his head after licking his whiskers and then sat to clean his face with his paw. "Because I have to eat before Mulder, Sparkles, or Wilber shows up. Perhaps now you might understand why I'd rather eat on the counter. At least I don't have to fight for my food there."

"Oh, and another thing, the theme of the ball will be the ghosts of Christmas past," I said. "That way we can get a little Halloween spirit going." I had other ideas for this plan, but I wasn't sharing them with Jasper yet. He'd try to talk me out of them.

"A place with no Halloween? Who would have thought? As a black cat, this month is usually my time to shine. I'm totally getting ripped off." He tipped his head back as he strutted across the kitchen tiles. "I'd better get a nice dish and some dinner after I work my magic by being my adorable self with Glenda."

"Even though you just finished eating, and it is nowhere near dinner time?"

Jasper narrowed his gaze. "Do you want me to do this or not?"

"Fine," I said. Most of the time, he decided that dinner was whenever he felt like it. It was usually at an inconvenient, or horribly early, time. He'd trained me well.

After Jasper left the kitchen, I went in search of Glenda and found her slipping back in from the balcony. She sure spent a lot of time out there smoking. "Hi, Glenda. I came to talk to you about the Christmas ball."

She yanked the curtains closed and crossed the floor toward me. "What about it? I've already taken care of everything."

"What do you mean? We talked about it, but I'm supposed to be... Well, *we're* working together on this," I said.

She shrugged. "I'm in charge of event planning. You proved you can mix a drink, but what do you know about planning a ball?"

"Plenty." I busted a couple of dance moves. "I'm practically the dancing queen at the nightclub where I work."

Glenda rolled her eyes. "I'm not talking about dancing. I'm talking about the planning."

I braced my hands on my hips. It might not be the same as a dance, or ball, or whatever she wanted to call it, but entertaining people and providing customer service was my thing. From the looks of the inn, it hadn't been Glenda's thing for a very long time. “How many dances have you held? Ones that were successful events?” I held up a hand. “Recently.”

“It's not a dance. It's a ball.” She paused. “Define recent.” Glenda circled the bar and pulled out a calendar planner and a stack of envelopes wrapped in a rubber band.

I picked up the envelopes and flipped through them. They were all unopened bills, dated from months before Mid died. “What are these doing here?”

Glenda shrugged. “Got me. I was going to give them to Grace. It might explain why Mid was behind on paying the bills. She never got them.”

I sighed and leaned against the bar counter, wondering who would hide the bills from Mid. Someone who wanted Mid to be forced to sell if she got behind on payments. Glenda wouldn't have given these to me if she was the one who had hidden them, unless she wanted to appear innocent. The only other person who I'd seen around this room was Sabina.

Had Sabina wanted Mid to lose the inn? Then became impatient enough that she resorted to murder? The housekeeper was very evasive every time I'd tried to talk to her—except when she offered me the spell that didn't go as planned.

Glenda lifted a piece of torn notebook paper, drawing my attention back to the current conversation. "I've already started my list for the ball," she said.

One glance confirmed that her list was long. Planning could go on all day, and I didn't have the energy. "Let me tell you my idea for combining Halloween and Christmas."

"It's stupid." Glenda closed the calendar and turned to walk away.

I threw up my hands. "You didn't even hear me out."

"Because I know stupid when I hear it, and sometimes even before that. Halloween and Christmas? Stupid," Glenda said.

"Grace gave me permission." Technically, she hadn't, unless I convinced Glenda to go along with my idea. This conversation was getting nowhere fast; I was going to have to be more persuasive to get her to agree. "Listen, I know it's an unusual idea, but that's our way of luring people in. Who doesn't like to dress up?"

"Plenty of people. Me," she said.

"Most people do, but it won't be mandatory." I smiled. "You could bring Sparkles as part of your costume. You could come as the craz—"

Glenda frowned, realizing where I was heading.

"Err, cat lady." I quickly dropped the word crazy.

I held my breath. She seemed to consider it. "I'm not sure Sparkles would go along with it. She doesn't like crowds of people. She's more of a one-person cat."

Jasper walked in with his tail held high and let out a meow. Glenda visibly brightened and bent closer to his level. "Who's this little guy?"

I cringed when she used the sing-song voice I reserved for Mulder. Well, until I had realized how much he hated it, although Jasper definitely hated it more. He cast me a narrowed glance before continuing with the charade of being pleased to be talked to that way. He approached Glenda.

"This is Jasper, my cat." I ignored the way Jasper hesitated. He was preparing to argue about whom owned who, but then he relented and allowed Glenda to pet him. "You could borrow him for your costume, if you'd like." I hadn't discussed that part with Jasper. Glenda's expression lit up, appearing to be enthralled with the idea.

She scooped him up and squeezed him until his eyes widened, and then kissed him on the nose. "Isn't he the sweetest thing?"

I gave Jasper credit for maintaining his cool. I just knew he absolutely hated everything about this. Or did he? Maybe it was only when I did it. He was permitting Glenda's attentions, and from the purring I heard, he might've even enjoyed it a little.

I stared at Glenda in fascination. It never ceased to amaze me how animals could bring out the good in most people. How by allowing us to love them, we became better able to love ourselves and others. Or at least it softened most people, as it seemed to with Glenda.

"Okay. You've sold me." Glenda snuggled Jasper closer. "Or at least he did. Although I don't know how keen Sparkles will be on the idea of sharing me with another cat."

"We've seen Sparkles a few times. She didn't seem to mind Jasper." I neglected to mention that it was because she had avoided him completely.

"We could make it a murder mystery theme with the ghosts of Christmas past." I clapped my hands together as if I'd just thought of the idea.

"That sounds awfully morbid." Glenda planted kiss after kiss on Jasper's head while he glared at me, hanging in her arms like a sack of potatoes with all four paws jutting out.

I'd actually thought that with Glenda's personality, she'd prefer something morbid rather than sweet and light. "It will allow us to display the history of the inn and talk about its future," I said.

Glenda looked to me with a slight smile. "That might be an okay idea."

"I'll leave you alone to think about it while you get to know Jasper," I said, giving the cat a quick wink before I left the room.

"THAT WAS TORTURE." JASPER LICKED HIS PAW AND ran it over his face to eliminate any saliva left from Glenda's kisses.

"You seemed like you enjoyed it." I hid a smile.

"I'm an excellent actor." Jasper trotted across my room to settle in his favorite spot by the window.

"Did you get any information after I left?" I settled into the chair. I hadn't found a better spot to talk to Jasper without risking the staff noticing my one-sided conversation.

Jasper scowled. "You mean did anything happen besides me being humiliated and treated like a stuffed toy?"

"Yes. Besides that," I said.

It was a long shot, but I hoped that since Glenda didn't speak to people much, maybe she'd prefer conversations with those of the fur variety. There were many that preferred that kind of one-sided conversation. She wouldn't realize that Jasper could understand her and convey any relevant clues from their conversation to me.

"She's not really a fan of yours. Not that I think she's a fan of anyone who isn't a cat. Mostly she complained, but I think she liked your idea for the ghosts of Christmas past dance more than she's letting on. She was excited about it. Maybe it's because no one takes time to talk to her and get past her rough exterior. She's not that bad underneath it all."

My brows shot up. "That's quite the psychological evaluation you've got going on there."

"It's common sense. Everyone wants to be heard. And she was afraid that when Grace came that she'd lose her job. She's worked here for over fifty years. What else is she going to do now that she's an old crow? Her words, not mine."

I nodded. "You might be right. Not about the old crow part, but about her worrying about her future. We need to show everyone that the inn isn't going anywhere, and that it's only going to get better. Grace needs this staff. They're the ones that truly understand and love this place and its history."

Jasper paused in his grooming. "Did Grace say she's keeping it?"

"She didn't have to. I know that's what she wants. Now it's up to us to help make that happen," I said.

Jasper closed his eyes against the beam of sunlight. "The impression I got from Glenda is that it might be good to shake things up a little. They've done everything the same way for so long. But, a Christmas ball at Halloween? I'm not sure how many would be into that."

"Exactly. A change might be what this place needs." I looked over his black coat with the little white patch at his throat. "I'm not sure why you wouldn't like a ball. You'd look cute with a little bowtie, with your tuxedo coloring."

Jasper let out a low hiss. "Don't even think of it. I've endured enough."

"It might be good to take a few of Glenda's ideas about the dance into consideration. How about Mid? Did she say anything about her?" I sat on the edge of the bed.

He looked away. "It was weird. She went out on the balcony to smoke, but thank goodness she put me down inside before that. Besides the secondhand smoke issue, it's pretty cold out there on the balcony. I'm an indoor cat now, you know."

Jasper never missed the chance to remind me of that, as if he was afraid I'd one day banish him back to the streets. That would never happen. Like

Glenda, under that tough exterior, he wanted to feel needed.

I nodded to keep him talking. He looked all introspective and might have had something significant to add.

Jasper continued. "She wasn't just smoking on the balcony. She was talking to Mid. I don't think she could see her spirit, or anything like that. I think she misses her. They had to have been close."

"What did she say?"

"She told her how we were planning the ball. That we might call it a dance to make it more appealing to young people. Then, all about me, of course. How much cuter I was than Sparkles—"

"Okay, enough with that. Go on about Mid." Most likely, he was exaggerating the part about Sparkles. Either way, it wasn't important. At least not to me.

"Then she said she missed her. It was sad watching her talk to herself out there, with no one answering. I actually felt bad for her. I wouldn't have complained if she'd wanted to pet me again, for her comfort, of course."

That ruled out Glenda as my number one suspect. Sometimes those strong feelings were dangerous, in that we unintentionally hurt those we love the most. Fear might have prompted her to act impulsively, and she regretted that later. But that wouldn't have solved her problem if the new owner didn't keep the inn and her. If I didn't find out who killed Mid soon, Grace could be in danger.

"That gives me an idea. Glenda might not see spirits, but I know who can: Mulder."

11

I sat in the corner of my room, observing Mulder. He returned an unblinking stare. When he suspected that dropping his guard could lead to something unsavory, like a visit to the groomer or the vet, he could maintain this stare for an extraordinarily long time.

"How can I replicate that spell?" I'd spent a restless night pondering this and now turned the small voodoo cat doll over and over in my hands.

Being shoved into Mulder's thoughts had been an accident. If I'd messed up the original spell, who knew if I could get the same results if I tried to repeat what I had done the first time.

I'd looked for Sabina to ask her if I'd messed something up when I'd performed it, and to get a sense if she exhibited any guilt if she'd intended for it to fail. But she wasn't working today, or she was avoiding me.

Jasper hopped on the bed, momentarily distracting Mulder from our face-off to look at the cat with envy. Mulder's short legs deterred him from his lifelong goal of getting on the bed without help.

"What's so important that you think you need him to help you?" Jasper looked to the dog with disdain. "Whatever it is, I'm more than capable of helping."

I tucked the voodoo cat doll out of sight and said, "Can you see ghosts? Or detect the scent of recently departed spirits to determine their cause of death?"

Jasper kneaded the comforter with his claws. "Who knows if that's even true. The dog might yank your chain to make himself seem more important to you."

Mulder narrowed his gaze, but it was difficult to tell if it was from annoyance, or because a ruffle on the edge of the comforter caught his attention.

"Besides," Jasper continued, "the spell could backfire, and you could succeed with your original intent to get into my head. We both know that isn't necessary *or* desired. Why don't you figure out a spell to talk to him like you can to me? Rather than transporting into someone's thoughts, which is invasive and creepy."

"I still don't know why I'm able to talk to you," I said.

He shrugged. "You don't need to do it for long. I've heard there are spells that might work for the short term. Isn't that all you really need? You always overthink things and make them more difficult."

I hated to admit it, but Jasper was right on the spell part, but not about making things more difficult. That was unintentional. I strove to make things easier for myself; unfortunately, I often failed. "Where do you hear about spells?"

"Everywhere. I hear things, and I know things. You don't give me enough credit." Jasper opened his eyes wider, which was his way of raising his brows to say something that was bound to be sarcastic. "You know who's good at creating spells?"

"I have a feeling you're not talking about me. My sister Ava's not here, and I don't want to bother her about this. She'd think I was looking for trouble." I leaned back against the headboard, clutching a pillow to my chest.

"Ava would be the best choice, but as you said, she's not here, and you don't want to involve Grace. How about Madame Ambrosia? Ask her how to get rid of that creepy voodoo cat doll while you're there," Jasper said.

He was right. Madame Ambrosia would be the

best person to ask—if she wasn't going soft, as Sofia implied. But that meant I'd have to explain what I wanted the spell for, and why. "She doesn't know me well enough. She'll think I've gone off the deep end."

"Not knowing about your lackluster spelling skills might be a good thing, and besides, you went off the deep end a long time ago." Jasper came to rub against my side. "Maybe she'd do it for Grace. Everyone loves Grace."

"Of course, they do." I sighed. I loved Grace too. I needed to do it for her, no matter how uncomfortable it might've made me.

"You don't have to tell her why you want it, only that you do. Make something up." Jasper flopped on his back and rolled around on the comforter, leaving a trail of black hairs on the candy cane images.

I sucked my lower lip between my teeth. "I don't know if she'll do it."

Jasper stopped rolling and flipped onto all four feet, shaking so the remaining loose hairs fluttered to the comforter. "Ensuring the safety of her great granddaughter will worry her. If there really is a murderer on the loose, I'm sure she'd want to do what she could to help the situation. To make sure that it's safe for Sabina to work here."

"Okay, but that's going to mean another trip into town, and I've gotten little started here with the decorations yet. Guess I better figure out how comfortable everyone is about magic, because that's the best I'm going to do." I shrugged.

"For catnips' sake, there are elves working here. You know it and *I* know it. How much denial can these people be in? We're at the Kringle Inn and the local voodoo priestess—or whatever she is—has a mailbox that goes straight to Santa's workshop. You don't think that people here are comfortable with magic? They embrace it every day."

"You really think the mailbox goes to Santa?" I regretted the question as soon as it slipped out, but Jasper only nodded instead of ridiculing me.

He had a point. There was a lot of denial going on.

"There might be another way. Maybe I don't have to be in Mulder's thoughts and talk to him. Perhaps I only need to see what he does. Remember the spell I performed to eavesdrop on Joe and Sully?" The secrets revealed might not have been what I wanted to hear, but the spell had worked.

"The spirit might still linger around if it—I mean, Aunt Mid—was murdered," I said. "They stay if they have unfinished business in this world. Being murdered and knowing someone is trying to force Grace to sell the inn would definitely be unfinished business." Maybe. Most of what I'd heard about spirits and ghosts was from novels and scary movies. It was possible there was fact mixed in with the fiction.

"That might be safer. Goddess knows that dog can probably see much better than you with his enormous eyes. Those peepers creep me the heck out at night. They glow like a darn jack-o'-lantern." Jasper narrowed his gaze. "Wait a minute. Do you mean you're going to do the spell instead of asking Madame Ambrosia?"

I smiled. "Sure. This one should be easier, and less risky, than using a voodoo dog since the cat doll didn't seem to work." I laughed, but neither Jasper nor Mulder appeared amused. "What? It'll be fine."

"How will it be fine? Let's say by some miracle you're able to make this work and you can see what Mulder does. How do you know you're going to see anything more than the floor when he's looking for crumbs or something shiny?"

Mulder growled low in his throat.

I pointed at him. "See? He understands more than you think. Don't let that clueless expression fool you. And besides, all things shiny distract you. Once the spell works—"

"If."

I rolled my eyes. "Once the spell works, I'll ask Mulder to take me to the spirit."

"Suit yourself. You'd have been better off if you'd allowed me to help more with this case. Why in the world you think that dog is better at sleuthing is beyond me."

"You *are* helping with the case. You're helping with Glenda. Don't forget, we're still narrowing down our suspects. She knows what goes on here better than anyone and could be the key to solving this if she's not the culprit."

"Don't remind me about her. That woman pulled out those reindeer antlers, and I had to endure wearing them for ten seconds. I did it to help you with this case, I might add. Never would I ever permit that at any other time, so don't get any ideas. Even Sparkles was smart enough to refuse them."

I brightened. "Does that mean now you'll wear the witch hat I got you?"

"No. I wouldn't wear it then, and I won't wear it now. I am no one's plaything." He paused. "Although, the hat would be better than those antlers," Jasper muttered.

"What was that?" I leaned toward him.

"Nothing."

"Okay, then let's get started." Now that I had a plan, I was eager to put it in motion. If I could find Aunt Mid's spirit and confirm her murder, she might identify the killer. Then I could worry more about

Christmas decorations and all the things Grace thought I was attending to.

Jasper's eyes widened, and he took a step back. "What do you mean, let's get started? Now? This is a spell you've only done once. You got lucky. You don't have a clue about a potion, or whatever else, might be necessary to make it work again."

"That's because you don't understand magic. Magic is more than rhyming and throwing a bunch of items together. To make it work well and focus it properly toward what you want to achieve, most of that effort comes from inside. It's powered by emotions." I tapped my chest. "Magic is about putting your intentions and desires into play. That's why dark witches, who have mostly bad intentions, end up with nasty spells."

Jasper's gaze flickered to my hair. "How does that explain that black streak you couldn't keep covered in your hair?"

I grimaced and ran my hand over my hair. I'd forgotten about it for a while since there weren't as many witches around to remind me about my lack of spelling skills. "That's because of my ..." I sighed, "frustration, rather than ill intent. Emotions such as fear, anger, and frustration can tamper with the outcome of a spell. It's a very delicate balance."

I suspected Jasper feared if I ever figured out how

to get rid of the black streak I'd gained with the ability to communicate with him, we might not converse anymore. That it would break whatever spell I'd cast.

"Whatever. Save the magic lesson for another day and for someone who has opposable thumbs who could perform it." He flicked his tail back and forth.

"Sounds like someone is jealous." I reached to pet him, but he lowered to his belly to wiggle out of my reach.

"Nonsense. I have better things to do than worry about your emotional stability in spelling. We all know the risks there," Jasper said.

"First, I need something of Mid's." I peered around the room.

Grace had mentioned that Mid had chosen the rooms' color schemes and individual decor. Every room contained photos or paintings of her, or her mother, grandmother, or great grandmother. They had all run the inn at one time or another.

Mid had put her heart and soul into this place. She'd want Grace to run it. Even if she wasn't murdered, it was possible her spirit might linger to help Grace get the inn prospering again.

I took a framed photo from the wall and ran my hand over it to remove the dust coating the glass. The photo was an old black and white. It had yellowed and faded from time, but the joy in Mid's face hadn't. The Kringle Inn was at its prime in full holiday swing, and the hall was bustling. The faces of the guests in the photo were full of Christmas cheer.

"Now I need something of Mulder's." I patted the bed until Mulder came over and propped his paws on the edge. He sniffed my hand, assuming I'd called him over for a treat. "Not this time, buddy. I need to borrow your collar." I unhooked it and placed it beside the photo. After removing the collar, he shook his head vigorously. The movement traveled down his body to his hips to shimmy and escape through his tail. He peered at me with happiness and a twinge of wariness. He usually only had the collar removed at bedtime or for grooming.

I leaned forward to make sure I had his full attention. "I'm going to do a spell so I can see what you see. I won't be in your thoughts this time. "

Mulder sat back on his haunches. I did not know if he understood or cared about anything I said. Hopefully he did, otherwise I might spend the time getting a Mulder-eye view of the inn again. And hopefully, the spell would go as planned and I wouldn't end up getting someone else's view.

I shrugged. It wouldn't be the first time I was taking a risk. Taking chances was the only way to grow my magic.

After mixing the ingredients in my small travel cauldron, I waved my hand over the top. This resulted in small cloud gathering and rising to the ceiling.

I settled on my back on the bed and rested Mid's photo on one side of me and placed my hand over it. I held Mulder's collar in my other hand. After a few deep calming breaths, I focused on my conversation with Mulder when he told me about the murder and the spirits. I thought about how much I wanted to help Grace. Then I thought about Mid. She loved this place and her niece. She deserved justice.

My focus was on seeing what Mulder saw. After about ten minutes, the various distractions in my mind ebbed away. A pinpoint of light opened in the ceiling and grew. I turned to Mulder. He sat on the floor, watching me while tilting his head from side to side. "Once I say the spell, I want you to take me to the spirit."

He rested his head on his paws. I ignored the chuckle that had to have come from Jasper and closed my eyes.

The sound of claws crossing the floor softened when they hit the carpet in the hall and confirmed Mulder had left the bedroom. I sat and waited while studying the darkness of the inside of my eyelids. I repeated the spell.

"Spirits have secrets and a few I must know."

"Allow me to listen and see those Mulder will show."

I waited. Nothing. Maybe Jasper was right and this wouldn't work. Either I didn't want it badly enough, or I really stunk at spelling.

An array of colors raced across my vision. I sucked in a breath at their dizzying speed. They finally slowed enough for me to realize that the colors were the pattern of the carpet in the hall.

My first assumption was wrong, the spell had worked. I did it!

I was looking through Mulder's eyes without having to invade his thoughts. Who, unfortunately at the moment, was mesmerized by an unusual discoloration on the rug. It must've been from a recent stain. He shoved his nose deep into the fabric and sniffed.

"Mulder. Show me the spirit." Unfortunately, this spell wouldn't allow me to communicate with him, only to see what he was seeing. But I didn't think it would hurt to remind him, in case he could feel any of my thoughts or intentions.

Mulder either somehow understood my request, or got bored with the stain, because soon the low scenery of the walls was racing by. He moved down the hall and then up the stairs to the third floor. There were only a few rooms on this floor. Was he going to Belinda's room? Did he think she was responsible for Mid's death?

He picked up speed until he reached the doorway of one room. The door was ajar, and he crept in.

The room lay in shadows.

Mulder's tremor shook the scene before me.

The room was vacant except for a figure sitting in a chair in one corner, but this wasn't Belinda. She was the only current guest of the hotel besides us, and also, this person was dead.

12

My first clue that this wasn't Mid was that it was the spirit form of a man rocking in the chair. He didn't appear to have died from natural causes—not with a bullet hole in his head. And it may have been the reason his spirit lingered. He also appeared to be dressed for an earlier time period. His fedora hat, chained pocket watch, and vest had me thinking perhaps the 1920s.

Mulder backed away, but not before the spirit noticed him and smiled. It was hard to tell if it was a pleasant smile of welcome or an unfortunate leer because of the bullet hole placement. We didn't stick around long enough to find out. Mulder had regained his momentum and skedaddled out of the room.

He rushed down the hall and turned into the storage room. Sabina had the door propped open with her housekeeping cart. She was nowhere to be seen, but another spirit was hanging out.

Literally.

The woman hung from the ceiling with a sheet wrapped around her neck. Her clothing depicted a time decades later than the man we'd just seen. Her expression appeared bored until she noticed Mulder. She raised her hand in a wave, causing her body to sway from side to side. Mulder sat and stared at her for a few moments and then turned to leave the room, brushing past Sabina as he did so.

He turned back after exiting, and we saw Sabina adding towels to her cart from the shelf lining the wall. Her hand passed through the shadowy spirit without hesitation. Obviously, she hadn't inherited abilities for detecting the dead.

I wished I could've heard what Mulder had to say, but I'd validated one thing. He could definitely see spirits. I also realized I hadn't been specific enough in my directions. The inn was well over a hundred years old; it bound any number of spirits to linger. The spell could wear off soon. We needed to find Aunt Mid *now*.

"Mulder. We need to go to Aunt Mid's spirit."

He slowed in his pace in the hallway. He'd been preparing to go to another room. My view tilted from side to side as he appeared to be contemplating my request. Could he hear me? I couldn't hear his thoughts with this spell but maybe he could hear still hear mine. "The lady in the picture," I said. "The picture frame I was holding in my room."

Mulder sat.

"You know, the lady who has hair that looks like candy." I pressed the thought at Mulder while picturing Mid's image.

Mulder must have sensed my urgency, or he focused on the word candy. He jumped up and ran toward the stairs. Once he started down, my view bounced up and down as if I were on a trampoline. No wonder he hated stairs so much. If I had to endure this ride to get to my destination each time, I was likely to be sick.

When we arrived at the bottom and the world stopped bouncing, Mulder trotted toward the main hall. It made sense that he'd want to go to the balcony. Most likely, her spirit would linger at the place she had died. Although, someone else was lingering there.

Mulder scratched on the glass, and Glenda started, almost dropping her cigarette. She turned away to stare over the grounds and took a long drag from her cigarette, looking to be in no rush to return inside. Mulder scratched again.

Glenda reached over and opened the door. "Fine.

You can come out for a minute. But you're going in when I do." She observed Mulder as he stalked around the balcony to the doorway to Mid's old office. "You're that little dog that came with Marissa, right? You'd better leave Sparkles alone. Don't tease her or chase her around. I won't have it."

Mulder sat and studied Glenda and the spirit sitting on the balcony railing beside her.

The pink hair piled up on top of her head resembled cotton candy. The pattern on her dress, though faded in her current form, still appeared festive. I recognized Mid before I noticed the cat eye glasses she wore. In all her photos, the glasses were on her face, or hanging on a chain around her neck.

One good thing now was that she didn't look too bad for someone who'd fallen to her death from a balcony. I'd feared she'd appear much worse and might frighten Mulder—and myself—further.

As with the other spirits, Mid seemed aware that Mulder could see her. It must have been a lonely life to be right beside someone while they never knew you were there.

Mulder thumped his tail from side to side and panted his cheerful smile at Mid. She didn't seem to mind Glenda standing so close to her. If Glenda had been responsible for her murder, surely she wouldn't be so accommodating? Unless she went by the old *keep your friends close, but your enemies closer* motto.

"Mulder, how do you know if it was a murder?" I'd neglected to ask him these important questions. Like how did he detect the answers, and if he related it to scent, how could he smell a spirit? That made little sense. But nothing about this made sense.

Mid was nodding her head and staring at Mulder. Had she heard my question? "Can you hear me, Mid?"

She nodded.

Holy canoodles! This was going to be easier than I thought. "I'm Grace's friend."

Mid smiled at the mention of her niece.

"Mid, did you fall? Or did someone push you from the balcony?"

She nodded again.

Wait a minute; I'd asked her two questions. Was she agreeing to falling, or to being pushed? I rephrased the question. "Were you pushed?"

Mid nodded.

"By whom? Was it Glenda?"

Mid shook her head no.

That cleared one suspect from my list. "Then who? Who did it?"

Mid pointed off the railing.

"I know how you died. You fell from the balcony. I want to know who did it." No wonder ghosts rattled chains and made spooky sounds in the night. It might've been the only way to get their point across.

She pointed off the railing again.

"Was it Belin—"

"Why do you keep staring at me, pup? Are you hungry?" Glenda had finished her cigarette and put it out in the ashtray right through Mid before standing and occluding our view of the spirit. "That big-eyed, unblinking stare is unsettling. Come on, it's time to go in. It's cold out here." She rubbed her hands over her arms to warm herself.

"No! Wait!" I tried to stop Mulder, or Glenda, so I could continue my one-sided conversation with Mid, but it was too late. Glenda had tired of trying to convince Mulder to go in and scooped him up. The world flashed before my eyes, reminding me of one of those amusement park gravity-defying rides on its way up. My vision spun.

"Wow. You're heavier than you look." She grunted and shifted Mulder to a better position over her hip. "Marissa would fault me if something happened to you. No way am I getting the blame for that. Let's go, little guy."

Now I understood why it infuriated Jasper when I picked him up.

Glenda returned to the hall and set Mulder down

after she slid the door closed. He rushed back and scratched at it.

"Not now. I've got work to do." Glenda pulled the blinds on the door closed, bouncing them off Mulder's nose. "Speaking of which, where is your owner? Marissa is supposed to be helping with these preparations. She keeps coming to me with all these ideas and insisting she can plan the perfect ball, or dance, or whatever she wants to call it. She can say all she wants, but without actually doing anything, it won't happen. Between you and me, I think she's all talk. I'm of a mind to give Grace my opinion. Regardless of whether she's her friend, Marissa will go home, and I'll still be here. Who do you think Grace will listen to if she's in it for the long haul?"

I gasped and opened my eyes to take in the ceiling of the bedroom.

Jasper was right. Glenda could sure talk once she got going. I needed to get down there before she complained to Grace about me.

"Well?" Jasper said. He was partially responsible for losing feeling in my legs because he was lying across my ankle. "Did it work, or did you just take a nap?"

"It worked. This place is full of spirits, Mid was murdered, and it wasn't Glenda." I grimaced as I stretched out my leg and unceremoniously dumped Jasper on the bed.

"Wow. I didn't expect that at all," he said. "Usually, these magic endeavors of yours are way less productive. Perhaps the holiday spirit here is good for your magic." Jasper hesitated and glanced around the room. "Wait. What did you say about spirits? I hope you mean alcohol, like there is booze stashed somewhere from the prohibition days. You don't mean ghosts? That's really not my thing."

"Yep. Ghosts. You better get used to it because I met several. Who knows how many there could be in this old place. The good news is that they didn't care about us." I shrugged. "They might be friendly spirits."

"Might?" Jasper lifted his back and tail until all the hair along his spine rose a few inches. He pressed against me while his gaze darted around the room. "Friendly or not, ghosts are not something I care to deal with. Leave that to Mulder."

I rubbed my hands over my leg to stimulate the feeling to return. "Next time please don't use my legs as a pillow."

"What do you mean next time? Just how much do you plan to push your luck?"

"Hopefully, I won't have to anymore. Now, I need to get to the hall. Glenda is complaining about my lack of help with the ball, and Mulder's down there." I stood on wobbly legs, bracing my hand on the wall until I regained my balance.

"You're going to leave me here when there might be spirits lingering?" Jasper pushed himself between the pillows on the bed until his head was the only thing visible.

"You'll be fine. If you're worried, you could always go hang out with Wilber. Nothing seems to bother him." I glanced at Jasper when he didn't respond. He seemed to consider the offer.

"Or Mulder," I said. "He could let you know if there's a spirit around." There might not be a better time to build the bond between my two fur babies.

I took my time returning to the hall. Glenda was sure to be ready with complaints about my absence. I wanted time to mull over what I'd learned. Exactly what that was, I wasn't sure.

I took in the rooms I passed with a wary eye. How many spirits lingered here? Why did they stay?

It was uncomfortable to think a spirit might've been watching me at that very moment. I could only assume most were amicable, but what if they weren't? Could one have been responsible for Mid's death? Or Steve's?

I sighed. It was hard enough to investigate people that were alive, let alone spirits. The only way I had any inkling of their presence was because of Mulder, but I couldn't keep trying risky spells. Not just for concern about my safety, but for those that I loved—whether they were mortal, magic, or of the fur variety.

13

"It's about time," Glenda grumbled as I walked into the hall. "Did you come for your dog, or are you actually going to help in getting this party ready?" Mulder was still sitting at the balcony door, staring at the curtain.

"Hello to you, Glenda." I patted my leg and Mulder turned my way. He whined and started pacing back and forth in front of the door. "Come on, Mulder. You did great."

Glenda frowned. "For doing what? I haven't seen him chasing Sparkles yet, so I'll give him that."

I waved her off. "I meant he's a wonderful dog." And he was. I didn't give him enough credit. Most people didn't. His silly, adorable face fooled them. They didn't realize how intelligent he was.

I studied the hall. With vaulted ceilings and

internal balconies along the third floor, it was gorgeous, old architecture. *Old* being the key point. "I bet this room has seen a lot over the years. Do you think the inn is haunted?"

"Of course it is," Glenda replied without hesitation.

"Why do you say that?" I cocked my head to the side. Perhaps Glenda had abilities I was unaware of, although she hadn't seemed to notice her smoking companion on the balcony.

Glenda shrugged, her bony shoulders visible through the thin fabric of her top. "Because this place is about two hundred years old. It's bound to have lingering spirits."

I walked over to study the photographs and paintings lining the wall. "Were there other deaths here? I mean, besides Steve and Mid?"

Glenda narrowed her eyes, assuming her usual expression of annoyance. "I don't know. Probably, but I've never researched the history. You'll have to ask someone else. I dwell enough on the past." She paused. "Why does it matter?"

I turned with my hands on my hips. "What if I told you this place is full of ghosts?"

"What if I told you I didn't care?" she said. "If they're here, they've been here longer than I have, and they've never bothered me a hoot. Now tell me your grand plans for this party and how in the heck you think you'll be able to get all this done in time." She gestured to the room that needed *much* more than decorations. It needed serious repairs to get the lights and sound system working in time.

I sighed.

Glenda really was no fun.

I could stall no longer. Grace would lose the inn if she couldn't afford to keep it. I glanced back at the old photos on the walls. Everyone looked so happy in those pictures.

I stepped closer. "Are you in any of these pictures?"

Glenda tried to wave me off. "Probably, but who cares? What's the use of looking back? You can't change time."

"I know. I've tried," I said, and Mulder whined at my comment. Perhaps he remembered that spelling mishap. I clapped my hands together, ready to rid myself of my procrastination, even though I was a master at it. Planning had never been my thing. It might be time to change that.

"Ok. Here's how we're going to get this place ready. We'll use glamour." I raised my hands and smiled as I cast a glamour spell. The bar area transformed from appearing fatigued with dull, faded colors to festive with a tiny tabletop Christmas tree and lights strung along the shelves.

Glenda frowned as my weak spell wavered. This resulted in the bar appearing to shimmy back and forth between its current state and the glamoured state.

I shrugged. "Well, something a little stronger than that. I was just giving you an example."

"Wait a minute." Glenda stood in front of the wavering image with her hands on her hips. "You said you want some kind of mashup of Halloween and Christmas, right? Like the ghost of Christmas past?"

I raised my brows. Who'd have thought Glenda had actually been listening to me. "Yes."

"You might cast a crappy spell, but it got me thinking. Something like this is what we need. Your spell displays how the inn looked before, back in our prime, like the ghost of Christmas past, and then it shows us the present view."

"Okay." All those old pictures must have somehow influenced me to replicate the decor of those days. At least, that's what Glenda had seen in the glamour.

"Then we can emphasize how we're working on our future. Because the inn has never just been about the owner. It's for the town. You know that, right?"

She turned to me with a spark in her eye and a slight smile.

"Sure." I didn't know what she was talking about, but I didn't want to dampen her enthusiasm. For a moment, it almost looked as if she was happy. I wasn't sure what to make of her mood change. What was the catch?

Glenda walked to stand in front of a photo. She gently removed it and brushed off the dust as she returned to stand by me. She turned the picture toward me and tapped the glass. "There I am."

I gaped. "Wow."

Holy smack-arolla, Glenda was beautiful. She was smiling radiantly, beaming up at the face of a handsome young man.

"Time steals from you. It sucks. You'll see one day," she said, some of the happiness fading from her expression.

I squinted at the photo. It had to have been close to one-hundred years old. Witches didn't age like mortals did, so seeing Glenda's appearance now and comparing it to the timeframe of the photo gave me an idea of how old she must've been. My bet was that she'd worked here way more than fifty years. Most women lie about their age; some even lie to themselves. I figure there's no harm in that if it makes them feel better.

She sat on the barstool. "That's the one thing about being a witch. Even with just a touch of magic in your blood, you often outlive everyone you love. Sometimes even if they're paranormal, too. Except for the vampires. Angels and demons live a long time, but most don't stay in one place for long. They don't settle like we witches like to."

I went to place my hand over Glenda's, but she pulled it away, appearing uncomfortable.

She cleared her throat. "But why not turn back time for this one night? Pretend that things today are like they were."

"They can be that way again." I wished they could, for Glenda. I would've loved to see her smile like that more often.

"Not for me, but maybe for the inn." She gazed around. "We might restore that with the help of the workers."

"You mean the elves." It was time that someone admitted what was right in front of them.

She nodded. "Yes. The Christmas elves."

I did a little fist pump. "I knew it!"

"They aren't the same as other elves you may have heard of or encountered. Their job is specific to maintaining the magic of Christmas. Like I said, the inn is here for the town, but it's here for more than that. The inn's actual job is to keep the Christmas spirit alive. Not just for us, or Tinsel town. We're also responsible for the entire East Coast."

"The East Coast?" This was turning out to be a bigger responsibility than I'd expected. No wonder the holidays seemed to have lost their luster over the years if the inn kept the holiday spirit alive. "Why haven't you told Grace that?"

"She needs to figure it out. If I tell her, it's not the same as when someone believes. Magic is everywhere, and it's especially important for Christmas. You just have to believe in it." Glenda shook her head. "I don't know why I even bother trying to explain this to you. You wouldn't understand or care."

I thought about what she said for a moment. I wasn't sure what had gotten Glenda nostalgic. If that bit of my weak magic had helped her, I couldn't imagine what a real glamour would do for her mood.

"What does that mean for the inn? We're not at the North Pole—not that it matters." My laughter died at her sharp look. "Does it matter? Is there really something at the North Pole?"

"You seriously have to ask me that?"

"Well, um, yeah." I hadn't believed in anything about commercialized Christmas for a long time.

She narrowed her gaze. "Didn't your mother teach you any of this as a kid?"

I shrugged. She had, but I hadn't believed in it

much lately. I wasn't about to tell Glenda about the embarrassing taunts of my childhood. Guess that was what you got going to a school with mostly mortal children and not knowing how to keep a secret. When I'd babbled about elves and magic they were quick to trample my dreams with their interpretation of reality.

Glenda patted the barstool beside her. "Have a seat. Where do you think the biggest hotspot of magic is? There are several spots around the world, and the North Pole is the biggest one. They centralized magic there because of the smaller population of mortals."

"Why bother?" I said, recalling how hard it had been to try to get someone to believe in something that only existed in their imagination.

"Everyone needs something to believe in." Glenda smiled. "Witches have magic, and most of us have always known about it, but what if you were mortal? Wouldn't you want to believe in something unbelievable—to give you hope that anything was possible? Including one day, a month, or a season if you're lucky, when people smile more and are kind to each other?"

"But why are you ..." I couldn't say it, not while she looked happy being lost in her memories—or delusions; I wasn't sure which yet.

She raised a brow. "So cranky?"

"That wasn't the word I was going to use, but yes," I said. Glenda was the least jolly person I knew and one I'd have voted as most likely to hate the holidays.

She cradled the picture frame to her chest and sighed. "I got tired of trying to convince everyone—well, people like you, anyway—about what the Christmas season is all about and why it's important. About how we should practice the magic of Christmas not for only one day, but all year long. We used to get lots of tourists in town and as guests at the inn. All our efforts were worth it when we saw the look in their eyes. They saw the magic, and felt it, and we could only hope they took a little with them when they left to spread to their part of the world. Then the number of guests trickled off, and even the townspeople stopped coming here. They put on a good show, but most are barely scraping by. We can't keep selling Christmas cheer to each other. What's the point? We might as well give up."

If spreading Christmas cheer had been Glenda's job, she'd lost her love for it a long time ago. I couldn't blame her. Not when I could see her point, from what I'd experienced.

Even those with the biggest Christmas spirit often packed it up with their bulbs and wreaths once the month was over or the bills arrived. Overspending made many people regret purchases when they had to spend half the year paying them off. Then the cycle started again.

Glenda looked at me. "The inn wasn't this bad until after we lost Mid. Sure, it was deteriorating, but not like this. She was the brightest bulb of us all. She held the lingering magic of the holidays here. Once she died, things went downhill fast. *Really* fast.

That's why they sent in more elves, although they're only a temporary fix. We need something more long term to keep the spirit alive. Mid saw that spirit in Grace, but it's a lot of work. Grace hasn't been here since she was young and may not understand the responsibility. She might not want that." Glenda shrugged. "If she doesn't, and someone else buys it who doesn't care, or doesn't have the magic ... Well, at least I'll have my memories."

I looked from Glenda to the photo she held, which represented all that she'd lost. "Let's bring it back. I'll help you as much as I can, but honestly, I think a lot of this can come from you, Glenda. If you believe, maybe the inn will too."

"I'm not a powerful witch, and I don't have the magic." She barked a laugh. "In fact, I don't have any magic at all. Isn't it obvious?"

"I think you're wrong there. Magic comes from

emotions, and you love the inn. Your magic might show itself differently than you think." I took her hand and this time she didn't pull away. "You can do this, and you won't have to do it alone. I'll help."

Glenda smiled. "Well, I didn't get the event coordinator title for nothing. I had to work for it. Guess I can pull out those old skills, if they haven't gotten too rusty. Let's get ready for this dance."

14

I pulled my coat tighter against the breeze as I made my way to town. The air had gotten cooler in the week that we'd been visiting, but I still wasn't any closer to solving Mid's murder. Once during my walk, I thought I'd glimpsed a reindeer wandering among the trees in the woods. At this point, there was little that would surprise me.

Mid had shared how she had died, but not who was responsible. The possibility that I was wrong had entered my mind more than once. Mid might have taken her own life, or her death could have been an accident.

Could I have blown everything out of proportion to take my mind off spending another Christmas alone?

For a minute, I'd thought it might be different this year. That Sully and I might've made it work.

No use dwelling on what could've or should've been.

Before she'd died, Mid might've gotten stuck on her last memory, or something might've upset her. Mulder spent so much time in Mid's old office, or staring out onto the balcony. I suspected that Mid lingered in those places.

I knew little about ghosts, but I suspected Sabina's aunt did. Besides, I wanted to stop at the library to research the deaths at the inn to find out more about our lingering spirits.

First, a stop at Ready Readings.

The dance could connect all the dots... if I could pull it off.

My prior visit had prepared me, so I didn't bat an eye when Sofia came out with striped tights and a red jacket with big buttons and white fake-fur trim.

Although, keeping my mouth shut about it was another story.

Sometimes the words came out before I could stop them. "I'm not sure how you get people to believe a reading when you're dressed like that. You resemble an elf more than a fortune teller."

"Don't let appearances fool you. This is Tinsel Town. It's what people expect, and Christmas is all about magic." She twirled, and her jacket lifted with the breeze.

I waved a hand. "I've heard that a few times now."

Something had infected me with the Christmas shopping bug during my last visit to town. I would've liked to blame it on a spell, or other magic that might have sent me into shopping overdrive. Everyone I'd asked about this possibility had denied it, claiming that would be unethical. It would've been easier for me to believe that than to admit I'd bought the same tights Sofia was wearing.

Sofia raised her brows. "Back so soon? Have you changed your mind about having a reading?"

"What, are you saying you don't already know what I want?" I averted my attention to the mail slot, noting a letter stuck in the opening. I poked the corner that was sticking out, so the letter dropped in, and the mail flap swung shut.

Sofia crossed her arms over her chest, and her bell sleeves gaped open. "I know it's not a reading, but I can't figure out what it is you're seeking. I'm not a mind reader. You're a witch. You, of all people, know that magic isn't as easy as it looks, and sometimes our gifts manifest in different ways."

"I'm sorry. You're right." Hadn't I said something similar to Glenda? It was time I heeded my advice instead of shielding my discomfort with sarcasm.

"I'm being too harsh with you. Actually, I have a few questions about ghosts. I thought you might be able to help."

Sofia shook her head, jingling her earrings which were shaped like tiny bells. "Ghosts? I can't help you."

I frowned. This wasn't the answer I was expecting. I might've ended up spending the entire afternoon doing research in the library. "You didn't even hear what I have to say."

Sofia turned and walked toward the hall, gesturing for me to follow. "I'm no expert in ghosts, but Madame Ambrosia is." She parted the beaded curtain.. The dark hall loomed behind her. "Come, she'll see you. She's been waiting."

"Waiting for me? Why?"

I swallowed. Knowing this town, she was waiting because she knew I was already on the naughty list. She probably had a crystal ball with a direct connection to the North Pole and Ol' Mr. Claus himself—not the one at the police station.

My pace slowed as I reached the beaded curtain, and then I pushed through. This was what I had come for. I couldn't chicken out now. My bravado faded further, however, when Sofia gestured that I follow her down another hall.

They did not design *this one* for tourists desiring a reading.

There was no holiday decor here, and the walls were empty with dim lighting. It was the first time since I'd arrived that I hoped to see any kind of obnoxious decoration. It might've helped to decrease my unease.

The dark hall ended at a doorway.

Sofia opened the door. "Come on now, Marissa."

I reluctantly approached, feeling uncertain why this was making me uncomfortable. Sofia knew things. Did she know who the murderer was and was leading me right to them? I'd probably annoyed lots of people in this cheerful town with my tactless questions.

I took a deep breath and stepped past Sofia to peer into the room. An overwhelming scent of magic had me wrinkling my nose. The old woman had to be Madame Ambrosia, but she was nothing like I expected.

She sat on a recliner in a small living room. A game show on a television in the corner had captured her attention. She held up her palm to direct Sofia and I to wait until the host finished speaking.

After the contestant responded with the incorrect answer, Madame Ambrosia barked out a laugh, displaying a toothless mouth. "How could you have missed that?"

When the commercial came on, she gestured that we could enter.

"Grandmother, this is—"

"I know who it is. Don't waste your breath. Come on and sit down, Marissa." She pointed toward the dusty couch with her cane. "Go on now, Sofia. We'll be fine. I'm going to have a chat with the witch who hates Christmas." She lowered the recliner until her feet dangled a few inches from the ground. Her short stature was apparent even while seated.

I studied the snow globe where Madame Ambrosia rested her hand. The little structure inside the globe, and its surroundings, looked a lot like the Kringle Inn.

I cleared my throat and said, "Hate is such a strong word. I wouldn't say that I—"

Madame Ambrosia held up her cane and then smacked it on the floor with a loud crack. "Silent night and silent witch, please."

I snapped my mouth shut on my fumbling excuses. Christmas was growing on me since I'd been here, but now wasn't the time to push her with my slow change of heart. She probably didn't care.

Sofia hesitated, looking reluctant to leave me alone with her grandmother. After Madame

Ambrosia gave her a sharp look and gestured toward the door, Sofia leaned to whisper to me, "Her bark is worse than her bite."

I observed Madame Ambrosia returning her bite to her mouth. The dentures had been floating in a container on the small table beside her. I hoped Sofia didn't mean that comment literally. "Don't worry about me. I'm used to working in a nightclub with all kinds of paranormal. I'll be fine," I said.

Would I be? Despite her harmless appearance, Madame Ambrosia reeked of magic stronger than I'd ever encountered. Mortals wouldn't be aware of the scent, but I'd detected it as soon as we changed direction down the hall. Perhaps Madame Ambrosia's purpose was to protect the Christmas spirit that I'd spent most of my life downplaying, ignoring, or criticizing.

That wouldn't be good for me.

I perched on the edge of the couch. My muscles remained coiled and ready to spring in case I needed a quick escape. "Thank you for seeing me, Madame Ambrosia."

"You can drop the Madame while you're in my home and get to the point. I don't mind missing the rest of this show, but the one after is my favorite. You have," she glanced at the enormous grandfather clock in the corner, "fifteen minutes to have your say."

"Okay." I swallowed. "Sofia said you might know something about ghosts."

She folded her hands over her lavender knit sweatshirt that coordinated with the knit bottoms. The pant legs rose on her legs when she sat to reveal matching socks. "Of course, I do. I've been around long enough that the ghosts in this town used to be my friends—and enemies."

How would I explain myself without mentioning that I saw the ghost from Mulder's view? I couldn't think of any easy way to go about it. "I'm trying to solve the murder at Kringle Inn. Mid's murder." I hesitated, but Ambrosia didn't argue or disagree about there actually having been a murder.

"Go on."

"I did a spell so that I could see the spirits through my dog's view." I grimaced, realizing that even as a witch, I sounded like a kook.

She nodded. "Dogs can usually see spirits because they accept whatever the world presents to them, unlike people who try to rationalize things until they fit into their idea of normal. Dogs are a very accepting species. They connect with both paranormals and mortals. Spirits are a combination of both."

"If a spirit lingers, does that mean they were murdered? Or have unfinished business? What is it that forces them to remain in our world?" I threw out all the possibilities I was aware of, hoping Madame Ambrosia could confirm, deny, or point me in the right direction.

She studied her nails and nodded. “It was their world first, and sure, most of their lives ended undesirably. That results in them sticking around.”

I shifted on the couch to avoid a rogue spring from pressing into my behind any longer. “Do they stay where they died? Would all the spirits at the inn have died there if they're still lingering?”

“Not necessarily.” She brushed at crumbs that had accumulated on the shelf her bosom created. “Sometimes spirits go to where they were most happy instead of lingering at the place that was the unhappiest, or last, day of their life. It makes sense that there would be many spirits at the inn. It used to be quite the cheerful place for most everyone inside and outside of town.”

“What changed?”

“People stopped believing in the season's magic. As the magic fades, so does the inn. You can do all the repairs you want, but if people aren't spreading the joy of the Christmas spirit, the inn will eventually fall into disrepair. Like a toy, or the relationship with a friend you've forgotten, as you moved on with the tediousness of life. As if you'd outgrown them or didn't need them.”

I felt a little responsible for the condition of the inn. No wonder my staying there didn't please Nick. My negativity could've only made improvements more difficult and potentially undo the progress. But I was changing. That had to mean something.

"You're saying that all those spirits didn't die there? That they might be there looking for lost happiness?" A trip to the library to research who died at the inn might've not been necessary after all, and Jasper would be really unhappy to learn that our current residence might've been a ghost magnet.

She nodded and glanced pointedly toward the grandfather clock. "That's correct."

I frowned. Unfortunately, the spirits might've decided to linger and wait for the inn they remembered to return, which could've been a long time, unless we did something soon. "What happens if Grace sells the inn?"

Ambrosia shrugged. "It depends on what they do with the structure and who buys it. Although, I can't say for certain. I've been around a long time, but in all that time, it has always been in Grace's family. Their line of magic created the inn, and the town, and helped to fuel the holiday spirit for much of this side of the country."

"Oh."

That was losing a lot of holiday spirit. I thought

of the mysterious buyer who wanted to knock down the inn and put a modern structure there. Little did they know that the very act would destroy the fragile magic of the place, and possibly the town. Or they might've known that and not have cared.

Ambrosia looked at the clock. "Five minutes and counting." She picked up the remote and laid it on her lap.

"One last question. Was Aunt Mid murdered?" I leaned forward to rest my arms on my legs, eager for her to confirm my suspicions.

"Without a doubt." Ambrosia turned the remote in her hands.

Even though I'd suspected this all along, hearing her confirm it made the reality of what had happened more unsettling. Murder wasn't supposed to happen in a place made of joy and happiness. No wonder the inn was on its last legs. "Why do you say that? Do you know who did it?"

She shrugged. "I can't say I've given it much thought. Spirits pester me here all the time. I don't let it bother me. Dying is another step in the circle of life."

I thought of Sofia's comment about Madame Ambrosia's failing mind. "Then how do you know it was murder? Did you see it in that, um, snow globe thing?"

"Because heights terrified Mid. She never went out on that balcony once in all her life," Madame Ambrosia said.

"Maybe she jumped." I winced when she pierced me with a sharp look. "It has to be considered. She was far in debt, and the inn is falling apart; the pressure and responsibility might've gotten to be too much."

I thought of Grace. Keeping the inn might've not been the best idea. It would've been a lot of responsibility resting on her shoulders. Besides the cost and upkeep, she risked ruining Christmas completely if she didn't keep the holiday spirit alive.

"Nope." Madame Ambrosia tapped her leg with the remote. "That wouldn't happen. You didn't know Mid. She loved this town, the inn, and everything that came with it. She'd never give up on them, or herself. Even if the inn was no longer wrapped up in pretty paper or a nice bow, she wouldn't give up if there was still one person who believed. That would be enough for her."

"Enough?" I'd never been one to have enough. I was an all-or-nothing person and had trouble settling for anything in between, but perhaps having something was better than nothing.

Madame Ambrosia glanced at the television. The music changed to an upbeat theme song. Her show was beginning. She sighed and turned to me. "Think of the best Christmas holiday you ever had." She held up a hand, brandishing the remote. "Close your eyes."

I did as I was told, fearful I'd get smacked with the remote if I didn't comply.

"Say nothing yet," she said. "Think about it. It may have been a while ago. I'm sure you had at least one special Christmas in your lifetime."

I thought about my Christmases throughout the years until I could find one that stood out from the rest. "Okay. I have it."

"Picture it in your mind. The day, the people—everything. Tell me what made it special," Madame Ambrosia said.

I frowned, struggling to think what it was about that year that made it different from the rest. "I'm not sure. It was our immediate family and one of our neighbors. Mom invited the widow, Mrs. Wingate, over for dinner."

"What gifts did you receive?"

I concentrated on the memory. "I don't know. I don't remember."

"What do you remember?"

An image filled my mind. "The dinner table. Mom isn't that great of a cook. The food rarely stands out, but I remember Mrs. Wingate saying how she had planned to have a peanut butter and jelly sandwich. It overjoyed her when we invited her over." I frowned. "Although, she ate little. She said it was because it was hard with her dentures, but I think even she didn't appreciate Mom's cooking but didn't want to say that. She felt bad that she couldn't afford to bring a gift, so she brought one of her houseplants, a Christmas cactus, and gave it to Mom."

I smiled at the memory. "For a mortal, Mrs. Wingate was a whiz with plants." My smiled faded and I lowered my gaze. "That was her last Christmas. She died a few days later. The cactus bloomed that day. Mom said she thought it was because Mrs. Wingate had found peace."

"You're saying that was the best Christmas in your memory, and what made it the best was because you made one person happy. That it wasn't because of a gift or the food—it was due to enjoying the gift of kindness and friendship," she said.

"I guess so."

"That was Mid's motto. If she made even one person happy, she'd keep the inn going forever." She paused and then added, "Oh, and yes, the snow globe confirmed her murder." She held up her hand. "No, don't bother asking. The globe didn't tell me who did it."

I closed my mouth on that question. The snow globe might not have told Madame Ambrosia, but I thought she might've already known and wasn't telling.

"Oh, and just so you know. Messing with spells that reveal the spirit world can have aftereffects," Ambrosia said without taking her attention from the television. "The spirits have a lot to say and not many who can listen. They're always looking to find new people to talk to."

"Okay," I said, not sure how to respond. With Jasper already talking my ear off, I could only hope that spirits wouldn't start yammering to me as well.

More than one person loved the inn, so if she were still alive, Mid would feel like she was serving her purpose. Unless someone grew impatient waiting for Mid to tire of maintaining the inn.

15

I set the boxes of Christmas lights down with a thump. Grace insisted that we do as much of the decorations as possible in the old-fashioned way. Old-fashioned meaning without the use of magic. She said doing it manually would help to increase the Christmas spirit and a bunch of other babble about hard work and rewards.

I stopped listening after she started sounding too much like one of my mother's lectures about relying on magic. I think Grace worried more that I might've accidentally blown something up in my efforts.

Luckily, Belinda was proving to be a big help. Hopefully Glenda and Grace wouldn't notice that she'd invested much more time decorating than I had. But I had other things on my mind.

"Who would've pushed Mid from that railing?" I

asked Mulder, as if he would answer. Instead, he cocked his head from side to side when I spoke. Had he understood Mid when I couldn't that day?

"Don't even think about it." Jasper sashayed into the room, walking on his toes as if permanently affixed to high heels. He hadn't liked it when I made that reference before, so I kept that amusing thought to myself.

"Think about what?" I feigned confusion, but Jasper knew me too well.

"Of trying another spell to get into that pooch's head, or vision, or anything of the sort." Jasper bent to sniff at the strands of lights.

"Don't get any ideas about chewing on those wires. I've ruined enough of these." I held up a long string. "To answer your comment, no, I wasn't thinking about another spell."

He narrowed his eyes at me.

"Okay, I was. But I have to figure this out." I dropped the tangled mass of lights. "Mid's murder, not these lights. I swear, hanging Christmas lights is probably enough to turn most people off decorating."

Jasper batted at a few of the bulbs that had come loose, and they shot across the floor. He said, "Besides, who's to say that the third time trying one of your spells isn't the charm and you do some actual damage to that fat fur ball's limited number of brain cells."

Mulder let out a low growl and Jasper backed away a few steps. "You've always been a potion kind of gal, and not always a good one I might add, so you're chancing a major blunder with all this spelling."

I hated to admit it, and I wouldn't to him, but Jasper was right about the risks.

Mulder craned his head for me to pat him.

Something could've backfired and hurt him, and I couldn't chance that. I'd gotten so caught up in catching the murderer that I wasn't thinking about the dangers. "Guess I'll have to do it like the decorating—the old-fashioned way—and look for more clues."

"If you were around Glenda at all today—which I might add, I've had to spend far too much time with her," Jasper wrinkled his nose, "you'd realize your priorities should include figuring out the rest of the decorations and plans for the Halloween Christmas thing."

I waved a hand. "I can multi-task solving murders and planning merriment. Grace has the vendors lined up, and Glenda is on top of preparing the hall. Most of the town will be here. Everyone is eager to bring the Christmas spirit back to the inn. That, and they're probably seeing potential sales of their own merchandise, since most of them will have booths out front for one-stop shopping." I shuddered with the fear that before this visit was over, I'd end up with footed holiday pajamas.

Jasper gasped. "I've underestimated you, witch."

"I've already got a recipe for a new holiday cocktail special for the inn. All that's left is to help Glenda finish planning the music and drinks. Then ensuring they got the sound system working again."

I wasn't exaggerating about the preparations for the dance. Glenda had taken on the tasks with gusto. Most of the staff seemed excited to get the place fixed up. The long-term staff were trying to get it to look like it did long ago, how the newer staff had never seen it. The elves were working double time. I assumed it was because of their desire to finish up and return home. None would admit where home was —or that they were elves—but I knew where that might've been.

Now that Madame Ambrosia had planted the thought in my head about how the inn thrived on Christmas spirit, I could see it improving on its own with each little effort.

Speaking of which, when I looked down at the stubborn string of lights, the kinks disappeared, and all the bulbs were lit.

"Most of the town..." I thought about having all the potential suspects in one place and smiled. "That's perfect!"

"What's perfect? That you've got one string of lights going? You've got a long way to go yet." He nodded to Mulder, who was busy scratching at the large box of lights awaiting my attention.

"What's perfect is that most of the town will be here for the dance," I said, picking up another strand of lights. "It will be a way to observe all the suspects."

"What suspects? You ruled out Glenda. Who's left?" Jasper said and batted at another bulb. "And how are you going to have some sort of murder mystery during a holiday celebration?"

"The guilty party wouldn't be able to resist returning to the scene of the crime—they'd want to see how the inn was doing. I think the murderer is someone who doesn't want to see Grace succeed. If the party is hopping, they're bound to be on edge. Maybe it's the mystery buyer. I need to get Janice to admit who the potential buyer is."

"What do you plan to do if you find out who it is?" Jasper looked at me. "What if it's a witch?"

"So? I'm a witch."

"I mean a witch who is good at spells?" Jasper's eyes widened. "What are you going to do, run over and make her a cocktail? Or cast a spell and end up trapped in Mulder's head while leaving your body ripe for the picking, or I should say, for tossing over the balcony?"

"You're so morbid sometimes," I said.

"It's in my nature. Cats aren't just curious; we're realists. Besides, we have nine lives. We can take the risks, unlike you."

I considered what Jasper had said about a witch being the murderer. "If it was a witch, wouldn't you think that they'd have used magic, or a spell, rather than tossing Mid over the railing?"

Jasper hopped on a chair and curled up. "Why make something more difficult than it has to be? Besides, it could've been impulsive, or they knew Mid was a powerful witch and didn't want to give her a heads up. She'd be able to defend herself against most spells."

"But why was she on the balcony in the first place if she was afraid of heights?" This nagged at me. What would've gotten her out there? Mid hadn't been a small woman. It would have taken an effort to move her unless there had been magic, or a weapon, involved.

"There's something else you need to consider," Jasper mumbled.

"And what's that?"

He cracked an eye. "You're placing a lot of stock

in what Mulder told you. Just how reliable is he? The inn was also drowning in debt. Maybe she was looking for a way out?"

I shook my head, not admitting I'd considered that Mid might've taken her own life. Admitting the possibility gave it more weight. "I refuse to believe it."

"Just because you refuse to believe it doesn't mean it's not a possibility."

"It's not just me. Based on everyone I've talked to, and the things they've said about Mid, I can't imagine her doing that," I said, tossing the strand of lights down in frustration and choosing another one to work on. Apparently, my Christmas spirit wasn't strong enough yet, or this task should've been easier. "And if she did, wouldn't she have made other preparations for Grace to take over instead of leaving a mess behind? Write a note, or organize something?"

"Seriously? If she's thinking of ending her life, she would not make a to-do list first. Go to the store, fix up the inn, jump off the balcony." Jasper wiggled his whiskers. "If it was suicide, then there wouldn't be any life insurance for Grace to put into the inn."

I perked up. "Where did you hear about life insurance? Grace didn't mention that."

"That's because you didn't ask. You've been too busy running around trying to find a murderer. They listed the cause of death as accidental. She slipped and fell from the balcony. Grace came across the life insurance earlier today when she was digging through the pile of papers in the office."

"Well, that solves one problem. Grace should have the money to fix up the inn. Guess I'm absolved from the party and the decorations," I said.

"What?" Grace walked into the room with Wilber close on her heels. Jasper hopped to the top of the chair and raised his tail.

"We can use some of the life insurance money to buy new lights if we're decorating the old-fashioned way. Speaking of which, how about a combination? We're combining Halloween and Christmas. How about combining old-fashioned hard work and magic?" I muttered a spell and cast my hand toward the highest points of the room. A few sparkles rained down and then strings of lights appeared, strung along the walls.

I smiled until a spark shot out, and half of the lights extinguished. Wilber squealed and rushed out the door.

"Probably because I didn't want to risk burning down the inn." Grace raised a brow. "I'm going to get life insurance—eventually," she said. "Mid didn't have her policy with her other paperwork. Arthur said that she had life insurance, because he said he'd made recommendations about getting it ages ago."

I wondered again if Sabina had stashed the overdue bills under the bar. She usually picked up the mail on her way to work each day. Perhaps the life insurance paperwork had been with those. Why wouldn't she want Grace to get the money for the inn?

Grace shrugged. "Even that's not going to be enough. We still need this ball and all the holiday festivities to rejuvenate the inn. If I'm going to stay, we need to do more than dig Kringle Inn out of a hole of debt. We need to make it come alive for the years to come."

"You're going to keep it?" The desire to tell Grace the whole truth behind the inn and the Christmas spirit burned within me. I was terrible at keeping secrets, and this was a big one, but letting her know might've impaired her Christmas spirit. It could've become more of an obligation and responsibility than a desire. The magic wouldn't be the same.

"I'm still thinking about it. But I'm leaning toward yes." Grace twisted one of the red coils of her hair around her finger and then let it spring back.

"Because you're getting the money to help repair it?"

"Not just that," she said, gazing around the room.

"The money helps to ease the stress of wondering how I'll manage, but I'd been considering it before then. This was Aunt Mid's home. It's been in my family for... well, forever. I can't let that go. Family ties and bloodlines are important."

I couldn't argue with that. Witches embraced tracing family bloodlines and holding on to traditions—hence my tiny obsession with Halloween.

Grace smiled. "But it's more than that. I loved this place as a kid. Coming back made me realize it had been missing from my life. This is someplace I can make a real difference, unlike my other jobs. This would be more than a job. It would be mine. I plan to announce it at the holiday ball."

"If that's what you want, we'll make it happen. I want you to be happy." My smile felt forced and didn't meet my eyes. If someone murdered Mid, they wouldn't want the inn to recover. If they discovered Grace was going to keep it, they could strike again. She could be in danger. "Why don't you keep your decision to yourself a little longer?"

"Why? What's going on in your head?" She asked. "I can practically see the wheels turning faster than you're tangling those Christmas lights."

I looked to my hands and realized I'd been unconsciously twisting the strands. "I think people will be more supportive of the event if they feel like they're playing a part in bringing the inn back to its former glory."

And it would give me more time to figure out who had killed Mid. I could stop them before they got any ideas about getting rid of the inn and the last of Mid's bloodline—Grace.

16

I opened the door and Mulder pushed past me into the room. Jasper lay curled up on the bed. My room was one of a few that had a cat door. It was proof of the depths of Mid's love for animals ... or cats, at least. Mulder wasn't comfortable using the cat door since he'd briefly gotten stuck there the first time he went through it.

"Wilber might know something. It's time to mix a spell to try to talk to him," I said as if I actually intended to go through with this.

"You've got to be kidding me." Jasper sat at attention. "You've had ridiculous ideas, but this one takes the cake, or should I say, the trough?" He wrinkled his nose. "You think the pig might know something?"

I shrugged and sat on the edge of the bed. "It's worth a try."

"A try of what? You don't even know what you're doing when you've cast these spells in the past. There's no way I can let you try this." Jasper stomped his paw.

I acted as if I was considering another solution. "I guess you could talk to him."

Jasper rolled his eyes. "I told you. He had nothing to say. Who knows, maybe he speaks pig Latin."

I crossed one leg over the other. "That's your jealousy talking."

He twitched his ears. "Me, jealous? Of a *pig*? Please."

I held up my palms. "You still have trouble accepting Mulder, and we both know he is perfectly fine with you."

"Just because he was here first, doesn't mean he gets to be the alpha in the household," he blurted the words and then looked away.

I cocked my head. "Neither of you are the alpha. I am."

Jasper ignored me and continued to rant. "Or that he gets to be your familiar. That's supposed to be a cat. That's what witches do. They don't have a dog for a familiar."

"Witches don't choose their familiar; it just... happens. You know that. It's a connection." We'd had this conversation many times. Jasper couldn't grasp that the choice wasn't up to me.

"You're saying what we have between us isn't enough of a connection?" He pushed out his lower lip in a pout.

"I'm not saying that." Our ability to communicate was unusual, but as far as I could tell, it was because of a botched spell. Who knew if it might wear off one day? It wasn't natural magic. It was me messing with magic, but I couldn't say that to Jasper. I loved him and would love him no matter what.

Thank goodness for that, otherwise why would I put up with all his complaints and idiosyncrasies? I was sure he put up with a few of mine—because he reminded me all the time. "You're trying to change the subject away from Wilber. The role of my familiar isn't important now. What's important is helping Grace. Isn't that what the holiday season is all about?"

Jasper scowled. "Since when do you care about the holiday season? I thought you wanted to focus on Halloween. You haven't stopped complaining about Christmas since we got here."

I stood to run my finger along the wooden bedpost. It had an intricately carved design of a horse-drawn sleigh on a snow-laden path. "Halloween is about giving, as well. Don't people give candy and other treats?"

Jasper twitched his nose. "I thought you were always more concerned with the *tricks* part of the holiday."

I ignored his comment because it was true. I loved a little fun. "This isn't about me."

I moved closer to him on the bed. "Do you want me to try the second eye spy spell again and see if it works so I can communicate with Wilber? I just need to make a pig voodoo doll and get something of his. Although, as you pointed out, it could backfire, and I might end up in someone else's thoughts or get stuck somewhere." I shrugged. "I guess that's the risk you take for friends. You'd be fine if I didn't return to my body. You'd still have Mulder. Grace would probably let you stay. Then you'd have plenty of time to get to know Wilber."

Jasper's eyes widened. "Fine. I'll do it. I'll try to talk to the pig, if only to ensure I'm not stuck here tempted by tinsel for the rest of my days. My digestive system couldn't take it."

I smiled and patted his head. "I thought you might see it my way."

"You can be very persuasive. But you'd better stop patting my head now if you don't want me to bite your hand," he said with a growl. "I'll be lucky if the pig doesn't step on me."

"Could you start by not referring to him as 'the pig'? I can't imagine he'd enjoy a conversation with you when you start off on such a rude foot." I reached to pet him but remembered his threat and pulled back my hand to avoid a swat.

"Fine. Wilber. But I don't think it will help."

"While you're thinking of doing good, how about being nicer to Mulder? It would be wonderful if the two of you could lay your differences aside and get along for the holiday. Think of it as a gift to me," I said.

"For Halloween?" Jasper flicked his tail back and forth. "Or for Christmas? The Christmas holiday is actually two months away. That's a long time to tolerate a slobbering mass of fur."

"You might find by then that it isn't so bad. I've been in his thoughts—"

"So you *think*. Who knows what happened with that spell." Jasper settled on the bed and laid his head on his paws.

"I was in his thoughts; I could tell. I know him." I said. "Although, Mulder is much more eloquent in his speech than you think." I ran my hand over Jasper's fur. Despite his complaints, I knew he enjoyed it.

"Throwing around big words doesn't make him better than me," Jasper said.

I sighed. "All right, enough. Let's talk about how we're going to narrow down our suspects." Talking about the case would cheer him up.

"Who are your suspects?" Jasper asked.

"Sabina. She has access to every part of the inn, and to voodoo magic, or whatever it is," I said.

"What's her motive?" Jasper perked up, eager to be my partner in solving the case.

"She gets the mail. I suspect she hid the bills. She had access to the bar."

He nodded. "You don't know for sure that she hid the bills. Mid could've thought it better to have the bills out of sight and out of mind."

"I struggle with motive for Sabina. How do we know anyone's motives to kill? Especially someone like Aunt Mid? From what I understand, she was the sweetest lady who ever lived. Maybe Sabina was jealous of Mid's magic since she was a masterful witch." I thought a moment. "That could also be a motive for Glenda. She's pretty resentful of witches since she doesn't have any magic—that she knows of or admits to."

Jasper tilted his head and said, "I thought you ruled Glenda out? Besides, she should know from being around you that magic takes practice, and some people are born more gifted with the craft than others."

I raised a brow. "Very funny. Belinda is another suspect. She acts like she owns the place already. Jealousy could have driven her to it. She might even be the mysterious buyer Janice mentioned."

Jasper nodded. "I like that idea better. Anyone who has a pig for an indoor pet must be up to no good."

I rolled my eyes. "Okay, the next suspect is Janice. She's eager to list the inn again and could be counting on a commission."

"What commission? The place is falling apart, and wouldn't a murder in the inn bring down the sale value?" Jasper said.

"Not if they were going for a haunted inn theme."

"But they're not; that's just you."

I shrugged. "I suppose." I contemplated the suspects. The sound of Mulder's loud snoring from where he lay curled up on the rug rivaled that of an old man. "What do you think about Arthur?"

Jasper wrinkled his nose. "Other than being decrepit and smelling like ointments and creams that make my eyes water if I get near him?"

"Yes, other than that. As a suspect."

Jasper pondered this and said, "Maybe. Perhaps he wants the inn to close so he can retire. Some oldsters can't bear to decide to retire until someone decides for them. But I can't see him having the strength to push Mid from the balcony. The man can barely do the stairs."

"True." Jasper was perceptive for a cat. Or it could be due to his incessant nosiness which he referred to as curiosity. It helped to talk this through with him. "It has to be someone at the inn. They would have the easiest access to Mid," I said.

"You're forgetting about the construction workers working around here," he said.

"The elves?" I couldn't imagine a Christmas elf was capable of murder. "You're angry about the reindeer horns the one guy keeps pushing for you to wear."

"So someone confirmed they're elves?"

"Glenda kind of did, but no one said they weren't, either," I said, secretly hoping that they were.

"One of them could've done it for who knows what motive. Maybe they couldn't take any more of Mid's cheerful disposition. Although, that's a better motive for Glenda," he scowled. "She's one bitter woman. Why do you think I'm hiding here? I can't take much more of her negativity."

I raised a brow. "Her negativity?" This from the cat who never stopped complaining.

He nodded. "Yes. Can't you give her one of your cocktails to help her attitude?"

"She had one but claims it gave her indigestion. I blame the old ingredients, but now I've gotten fresh stuff. I offered her another one, but she was quick to turn it down. She doesn't know what she's missing. My cocktails can be fabulous."

"I have seen positive results," he said. "You have good intentions, just poor spelling."

"I wish Joe was here." I sighed, thinking of my hairdresser and undercover angel back in Florida. "He'd know what to do and how to narrow down the suspect list. He has a way of rounding up all the gossip."

"Or Burton?" Jasper offered. "He could scare the truth out of them with a single look."

"Demons are like that, but I don't think they'd really have a place here." I smiled. "I miss them, and Gran even more so. The Halloween holiday won't be the same without them." I nodded. "All the more reason to get to work."

"Doing what?" Jasper stretched out, not looking like he was getting ready for anything more strenuous than a nap.

"You need to talk to Wilber. I'm going to ensure everything is on schedule for the holiday ball. We need to do this to help Grace succeed."

Jasper sat up, and I held up a hand. “Don't worry; I'll be nearby so nothing goes wrong. Be careful about accidentally offending Wilber. I'd recommend holding off on those bacon jokes. It's doubtful he’d find them amusing. If you're working on Wilber, and I'm working on plans for the ball, we can kill two birds with one stone.”

Jasper cocked his head. “Would a stone work on killing a pig?”

“Like you'd ever do that. You're too nice. You just hide it under sarcasm.” I bopped his nose with my finger.

Jasper twitched his whiskers. “It's a curse being this cute.”

WILBER WASN'T HARD TO FIND, WHICH WASN'T A surprise. His size made it difficult for him to conceal himself anywhere for long. Perhaps Belinda had thought he was one of those cute potbellied pigs when she adopted him. They made the perfect pet until they continued to eat everything in sight and never stopped growing. And Belinda wasn't putting many restrictions on Wilber's diet.

“There he is,” Jasper whispered, as if I hadn't

noticed the pig in the library. What he was doing there was the question.

"I'm not bringing in those truffles," Jasper hissed. "It's an insult. You tell me to lay off the pig jokes, yet you assume the only way he'll talk to me is by offering food. What if I can't get out of the way before he snarfs it down? Have you seen him eat? That boy can do serious damage to a plate of food in record time. I'm not taking the risk."

"Suit yourself. I'll go sit by the window while you have a chat. I won't be far if you need me." The library was lovely and could be even more so with a little love and attention. I settled into the sofa by the window and picked up a magazine.

I could only hope that Glenda or Grace wouldn't walk by and see me lounging. I'd promised to help Glenda, so it would irritate her. And I couldn't tell Grace about my plan to talk to Wilber; she had already tired of my obsession with solving murders. Her words, not mine.

Although, Grace popping in the library was less likely now since she'd finally gotten a reprieve from Wilber. The pig had taken to her like he'd imprinted on his long, lost mother. Grace tried to shake him to avoid Belinda's jealousy. Until now, Belinda never had to compete for Wilber's affections. From his size, it appeared her way to his heart was through his belly.

I glanced at Jasper. He was quietly making his way toward Wilber. Jasper hadn't complained about my lingering, nor insisted I work with Glenda. He'd never admit it, but he was afraid of the pig. I wasn't sure why. The cat acted like he had so much attitude around every other animal he encountered. Since he was born in Florida, he hadn't met a pig before. Mulder and I had lived in Pennsylvania before moving to Florida, so seeing pigs was more common. Maybe that was it.

"What are you doing?" Jasper said to Wilber.

I stopped turning the pages of the magazine, featuring festive holiday decorations I hoped would inspire me. Jasper may have made the comment as a conversation starter, but the tone sounded accusatory.

Wilber snorted and raised his snout. A quick glance confirmed what I'd suspected. He'd found something to eat, though newspapers weren't usually edible.

"I apologize. We started off on the wrong foot." Jasper's voice sounded tight and uneasy.

Wilber raised his head and squealed. Jasper joined in with a shriek.

17

"Wait. I brought you something." Jasper darted across the room and around the corner to pick up the discarded truffles. He returned to drop them at Wilber's feet and then retreated.

Wilber oinked, and shreds of newspaper fell from his mouth. A few strands of paper stubbornly remained, clinging to his lower jaw. Despite Jasper's discomfort, Wilber didn't appear the least interested in stomping him to death. He only seemed mildly interested in Jasper and much more interested in the truffles he'd already inhaled.

The pig snorted and shook his head about. I couldn't tell if he was excited or irritated that the food was already gone. Jasper jumped on the coffee table, probably as a precaution. "Did you see anything on the night Mid died? The lady that owned the inn?" He must've decided to ditch the small talk and get right to the point.

Wilber quieted and stared at Jasper.

"She's the one with the big, pink hair. It looks like cotton candy. Maybe like food?" Jasper spoke quickly to keep the pig's limited attention.

That got a reaction out of Wilber. He squealed so loudly that Jasper jumped at least three inches off the table. I hid a snicker. I'd determined one reason Jasper preferred not to talk to Wilber. Each time he squealed, Jasper sprung into the air like he'd heard it for the first time.

Jasper shot me a nasty look, and I dipped my gaze back to the magazine. He'd seen my reaction. I would be hearing about this later.

"Can you describe her? What did she look like?" Jasper sighed when Wilber let out a few grunts and snorts. "How do I explain this to you when you only think in terms of food? Was her hair the color of corn? Or potatoes? Or... I don't know. Tell me what you remember," Jasper spoke quickly, alternating between flattening his ears and pitching them forward.

Wilber let out more squeals and then lost interest in the conversation. He trotted toward the exit. Jasper backed dangerously close to the edge of the coffee table to avoid getting tossed off when Wilber rammed the side in his haste to exit.

I returned the magazine. It had given me a few ideas for decorating. "Well, how did it go?"

"How did it go?" Jasper stalked across the floor toward me. "What did it look like? You owe me big time."

"Why? Because Wilber's voice hurts your ears?" I covered my smile with my hand.

"You have no idea." He shook his head. "I may have blown out an eardrum. It's like talking to a dog whistle when he gets to that volume."

"Did you learn anything?"

"Besides the fact that he relates everything to food? I feel dirty from being close to that animal." Jasper began frantically cleaning himself. "Do you have any idea how hard it is to have a conversation using food as references to figure out what he's talking about?" He paused in his bathing. "He confirmed Mid's murder."

"Really, how? And why didn't you start with that?" Relief washed over me. Not about the murder. No matter how tragic, there was nothing that could've changed that. My earlier spell with Mulder had worked! Proving he wasn't one bone short of a rack, as Jasper liked to say.

"I needed time to compose myself." He ran his

paw over his face. “It was challenging to get any details. Luckily, Mid had been eating not long before she died. She gave Wilber scraps when he ate, so he lingered. He was following her, hoping she had something else to give him when she went to the balcony with someone. The person had something with her in a bag. It wasn't food, so Wilber didn't really know, or care, what it was. But when a woman pushed Mid over the balcony, it upset him.”

“Her? How did he know it was a woman?”

“Well, unless Arthur or the workers start walking around on those foot coverings with the long pointy thing that echoes off the floor, then it was a woman,” Jasper said.

“Heels?”

“That would be my guess. Wilber was familiar with the sound since Mid always wore heels. He'd track her down in the hotel by following the echoes on the wood floor to see if she had any snacks for him.” He cocked his head in thought. “Unless he was referring to Mid's heels and not our killer. Then it could be a man.”

“Who was it? Who murdered Mid?”

“I don't know,” Jasper said. “He couldn't describe her, so I couldn’t understand. I mean, I was trying, and failing, to figure out if she was a blonde or brunette by comparing it to descriptions of food.”

I raised a brow. "Corn or potato? That's what you were trying to do? Determine hair color?"

Jasper hopped up on my lap. "Do you have a better suggestion of something a pig would be familiar with? Nothing prepared me to talk in culinary lingo to identify a murderer."

"You did good. We made progress." I ran my hand down his back. Even if he wouldn't admit it, the encounter with Wilber had stressed him.

He arched his back against my hand. "I'm not sure I'd call that progress."

I scratched him behind the ear. "We know it was a woman, and she brought something for Mid."

"That could've been anything," he murmured, closing his eyes while I continued scratching.

"It was in a bag," I said.

"That really helps," Jasper said with a trace of sarcasm.

I paused and turned toward the door. Someone was coming. The rapid pace, increasing in volume, alerted me they were on their way to the library. Most likely, that would be Glenda.

It wasn't.

Janice peered around the library, which was empty except for Jasper and me.

"Hello, Janice."

"I thought I heard you talking to someone," she said and raised her brows. "I was looking for Grace."

I forced a laugh. "Just talking to myself, and Jasper is a good listener."

Her brows pulled down as she studied me, and then she turned and walked away.

I stood. "I better go work on the preparations for the dance. If Glenda finds me sitting around, I might be the next one murdered."

❧

IT MIGHT'VE BEEN OCTOBER 31ST, BUT THE Kringle Inn looked more like Christmas had arrived than Halloween, and I was okay with that. The twinkling lights in the trees added to the illusion.

I parked Grace's car at the end of the lane. There was little chance of getting any closer with so many vendors lining the front of the inn. I stepped out of the car to admire the scene. The twinkling lights strung through the surrounding Christmas trees helped it to truly looked magical.

There was a station for hot chocolate and other food vendors from town. Giggling drew my attention to the craft tables that were scattered about. Kids were stringing popcorn or decorating stockings and playing games such as pin the nose on Rudolph or the reindeer antler toss.

As I started up the lane, I stepped aside so several people dressed as Santa could hurry pass to make it to the Santa costume contest judging.

Despite reassurances that there were no spells cast to loosen the inhibitions of impulsive buyers, I avoided the tables selling items from the shops in Tinsel Town. I had plenty of Christmas attire. Although, I thought the matching holiday pajamas might've been cute for Mulder and Jasper. Just as long as *I* didn't have to wear them, as well.

An ice sculptor had already completed several figures. They lined the walkway in front of the house. People stopped to watch while he worked on another. Since we'd gotten the sound system repaired, we could pipe the holiday music throughout the inn and outside. I even threw a few Halloween songs into the mix.

The only thing missing was snow. I would have thought that would be the easiest part, but Grace insisted we weren't using magic to mess with the weather. I supposed she was right. There were likely wicked consequences in messing with Mother Nature. If we failed to summon her, we could risk bringing a weather element witch out of the woodwork. They were discrete but very territorial.

I approached Grace and engulfed her in a hug, putting her on the receiving end of the surprise embrace for once. "This is wonderful."

"Isn't it? And don't worry, Halloween is still going on in the hall tonight. Wait, I mean Hallow-Christmassy, or whatever it is." Grace laughed.

I shrugged. "I don't know. Christmas is growing on me. I didn't realize how many shops there were in town until you got almost all of them set up on the front lawn." I scanned over the vendor stands and stopped. "Isn't that Janice at the beauty product booth? I thought she was a realtor?"

"She is, but she has other little businesses she does on the side. She's been trying to sell me products. Some of them are pretty good." Grace averted her gaze as she always did when she was lying. She'd never say a mean thing about anyone.

"For a mortal?"

Grace sighed. "I hate to put it that way, but yes. I'm sure it's hard to compete with products that have a touch of magic, but most of those are illegal to sell to mortals, anyway."

Potions were my thing, so I was curious what she was selling, even if the products weren't magically enhanced. "I'll look. They could make excellent gifts."

"Marissa." Grace's voice was stern. "Don't get any

ideas about adding magical enhancements to her stuff."

"I'd never do that." With a wink, I walked over to Janice's table. She'd filled it with various face creams, bath salts, candles, and lotions. I picked up a body spritzer, wondering if this might be a new way for me to distribute potions without putting them in a cocktail.

"Hi, may I interest you in a free sample?" Janice extended a bottle of hand lotion and squirted it on my arm before I could refuse.

"Oh, sure. I'm just looking, though." I wrinkled my nose at the overpowering scent of the lotion when I rubbed it into my skin. The potent scent confirmed they made it for mortals. Witches had sensitive olfactory senses, so they infused any products made for them with only the mildest of scents.

I tried to disguise my distaste, trying not to offend her. I felt bad about the initial impression I'd made on her the night we had arrived, but unfortunately, my first instincts had been correct. This stuff was terrible. I couldn't imagine she could sell much of it, even to mortals. "Thanks. You have all kinds of things here, but I better get inside and give Glenda a hand."

"Stop back later if you want to try something else. Or I can come over another day if you'd like. A woman can never have too many pampering products." Janice held up various lotions and powders and shook them at me as if it would lure me back.

I hurried away with a smile and made a quick stop at the bathroom to wash off the lotion before heading to the hall.

I gasped when I entered the hall. "This looks even better than I expected." I took in the transformation. I'd seen most of the decorations earlier that day, but something about the low lighting and the final touches had brought it all together. Glenda must've been responsible for those finishing touches, even if she wasn't aware of it.

"What? You didn't think I still had it in me?" Glenda huffed as she tugged at the hem of her dress and gestured to Jasper. "Come on, little kitty. You need to stick with me to make my costume authentic."

I kept my mouth closed since her costume didn't look like anything other than dressing up a little more than usual. Jasper was probably serving as more of an emotional support animal for her tonight. Although, compared to her usual garb, Glenda looked stunning, so perhaps it was a costume after all.

I looked to the ceiling. "The disco ball is great."

Glenda rolled her eyes. "I don't know why you needed that. We already have a hodgepodge of decorations for Halloween and Christmas. What's the point of throwing in a disco ball?"

"We just need one. You'll see. It will help get people in the mood to dance." The magic I'd used to make the ball included a few special devices, thanks to Nick. I presented my requests as a need for extra security, and not for spying on any guests who might be the murderer. I'd only use it if I needed to record a confession. We'd have the case solved long before that—hopefully.

I kept glancing toward the balcony, wondering if Mid lingered there, and if the guilty person would visit the scene of the crime.

With a harrumph of disapproval, Glenda walked away as guests arrived. Many had embraced the idea of a costume party, which made it hard for me to identify people. "Uh oh."

My idea might've backfired. I squinted at a couple walking in dressed as Santa and Mrs. Claus and another following as a candy cane and a Christmas tree. I realized too late that costumes would make it difficult for me to pinpoint the culprit if I didn't recognize them.

Most of them walked right through the doorway without hesitation, but Nick stopped. He looked at the charmed cocktail I'd made special for him and then directly above him, where I'd hung the mistletoe.

Grace approached right on cue after my text, letting her know Nick needed something in the hall. She stopped to talk with him. After a few moments, she looked up.

The mistletoe and the mimosa might have contributed to the magic, but I didn't think they would've needed either. It was obvious they belonged together. Sometimes it just takes someone else giving love a little nudge. Nick and Grace kissed and then moved aside to let others enter the room.

Another couple entered wearing disco attire from the 1970s, although the colors of their costumes—and their complexions—were faded and grey.

I smiled. A few of the ghosts of Christmas past had arrived.

Next, I needed to check to see if the treat I'd arranged for Glenda was working out.

18

"Glenda. There's someone I'd like you to see." I rushed up behind her.

She sighed. "Who? I think I've already talked to everyone from town at least three times, and also people I don't know. I'm all peopled out."

I waved her over. "You'll want to see this guy. He's only here for one night."

Glenda frowned. "Now you're being cryptic. This better not be a trick. I have no patience left."

Jasper wound around her legs, and she picked him up. I was grateful he sensed her unease and was here to help comfort her.

I led Glenda down the hall outside of the ballroom that led to the rooms. The twinkling lights provided enough illumination for us to find our way. I stopped in front of one of the guest rooms. "Are you ready?"

"For what? We need to get back. Sabina can only hold things down at the bar for so long." She rubbed her hand along the side of her neck.

I put my hands on her shoulders, then dropped my arms to my sides when she pulled away. "You know what night it is tonight."

Glenda rolled her eyes. "Of course, all I've heard about is this Hallow-Christmassy or whatever you want to call it. Like I could forget."

"No, not that. Well, it is that night, and the dance is a big hit, I might add. But it's also Halloween. The most magical night of the year." I took her hand in mine and squeezed it.

She sighed. "Oh, for goddess' sake, I stopped celebrating that ages ago. Are you going to make me bob for apples? Carve a jack-o'-lantern?"

Darn it. Those were enjoyable activities. I could've included those with the outside festivities. Leave it to Glenda to start sharing her ideas at the last minute. "No. Nothing like that. You've been thinking mortal thoughts for far too long. You're a witch."

She shook her head. "Not much of one, and not for a long time."

"I don't mean you have to be practicing the craft.

You understand the true meaning of Halloween. All Hallows Eve precedes All Hallows Day. It's when the veil that separates people from the world of the spirits is the thinnest. It's when sometimes—"

"I know, I know. Many can see the other side. I'm not here for an educational lesson about Halloween. Are you doing this because I was telling you about Christmas? Is this to show me you know about Halloween?" Her brows shot up. "Wait. The world of spirits. Are you saying some guests at the party weren't really guests?"

I nodded. "They're still guests, only from long ago. They've been waiting a long time to come out for a party like the old days."

Glenda paled and clutched Jasper tighter until he let out a squeak. She turned to glance toward the room. Her hand strayed to reach up and pat her hair as if it had suddenly gotten out of place, despite layers of hairspray. "Guests from long ago?" She met my gaze.

I nodded.

"I ... I'm not sure I'm ready." Her eyes were bright with moisture.

"Come on." I thought she might've grasped what was happening by now. Perhaps part of her had suspected or hoped when we were planning the dance. That might've been why she was wearing the dress from the picture on the wall. Time might not have been as kind to her as the dress, but it still looked great on her. "You look perfect." I threw open the door and stepped aside when she gasped.

He stood from where he'd been sitting and pulled the fedora lower to conceal the bullet hole. A bright light shimmered around his form.

"Ernie?" She turned to me. "But how? This isn't a trick, is it?"

I shook my head and laughed. The joy I felt emanating from Ernie, and now Glenda, was the best treat I'd ever gotten. "I just told you how, and no, I'd never trick you with something like this."

Glenda put her hand over her trembling lips. "But after tonight, he'll leave again, won't he?"

"I don't know. Probably. But who are we to worry about tomorrow? Magic is in the air. Let's enjoy tonight." I pulled Glenda into an awkward hug, and she didn't resist.

"Thank you." She handed me Jasper and stepped through the doorway and into Ernie's arms. I closed the door softly behind me and leaned in to whisper to Jasper. "One good deed down. See? You thought I didn't like to give treats."

"Who would've thought you had it in you?" He purred.

I gave him a little squeeze. "You knew I did."

"Yes, I did. That was nice to see. Will Ernie and the other spirits move on after this?" Jasper said.

I shrugged. "They're not so bad, huh? I know little about spirits. Maybe they'll stay, since this is their happy place?"

I quieted when I noticed Janice peering down the hall our way. She turned and went the other way. I shook my head, not caring that she probably thought I was talking to myself.

Jasper shifted in my arms and I ran my hand down his back and said, "Anyway, I'm not an expert on ghosts, as we've confirmed time and time again," I said. "But as I always say—"

"I know, you'll worry about that tomorrow." Jasper rubbed his head against my chin. "Come on, witch. Don't we have another good deed to do? We've got a killer to catch."

I STEPPED OUTSIDE TO THE PORCH AT THE entrance to the inn to survey the people milling around the grounds.

"I can't believe I'm saying this, but I think your Halloween Christmas dance, or whatever you are calling it, is a success," Belinda said with a smile, lifting her glass. “Finally, someone is able to care for the inn like it deserves.”

“Thank you,” I said.

Belinda narrowed her gaze at me. “What? Oh, sure.”

Apparently the complement wasn’t for me. I glanced at her glass. “Are you enjoying your specialty cocktail?”

Belinda hiccuped and placed a hand over her mouth. “Oh, my. Yes. What did you call this again? I can't say I've ever had something so delicious before.”

“It's a Merry Mistletoe Mimosa. You wouldn't have had it before because it's one of my specialty cocktails.” I kept a light hand on the charmed ingredients for Belinda since she was a mortal. Mortals could have unpredictable reactions to potions, but it looked as though it was having the right effect on her. I'd never seen her so merry.

Wilber trotted over to stand by Belinda. “Someone else is in the holiday spirit,” I said.

“He's embracing both Halloween and Christmas. Isn't he adorable?” Belinda reached down to pat him on his head behind his Santa hat.

“He is,” I said. He was also wearing a spider costume with two extra legs jutting out on each side. It made for a very odd-looking combination. At least he didn't mind the hat or the costume, unlike my fur family, who objected to wearing anything.

Belinda sighed. "Do you think Grace will take over the inn? Or sell it?"

I studied her. "I don't know if she's decided yet. Why?"

Belinda shrugged and looked behind her to study the inn. "Someone from town has always run it. An outsider can't love it like we do."

"I wouldn't call Grace an outsider," I said, while wondering if Belinda thought she might've been a better innkeeper. "They've handed the inn down through her family, and Grace loves everything about it."

"Then how come she hasn't visited in years? She can't love it *that* much. Not like me, or even Wilber here. She might not let him have the run of the place like Mid did." She pet Wilber, and he snorted on cue, although he had his head buried in a pot of poinsettias. He raised his snout, and chunks of dirt fell from it.

"That will be up to Grace—whether she wants to keep it, and how she wants to run it." We watched as Wilber trotted down the steps into the crowds of people, most likely looking for food and potentially scaring off a few guests. I liked the pig, but he might not always be good for business.

I'd heard as much from Jasper when he had reported in on the household gossip. Apparently, despite Mid's love of animals, even she had gotten frustrated with Wilber and the damage he'd done at the inn. It might've not thrilled all guests to share the inn with a pig who ran wild through the whole place.

Belinda held the rail as she descended the steps of the porch, calling for Wilber as she went. He'd gone directly to Grace, as I'd expected. The pig knew what side his bread was buttered on. He was probably trying to get on her good side to ensure he maintained his welcome.

I walked to stand beside Grace. "And you always say I'm the one that attracts all the animals." I nodded toward Wilber. He made a beeline back to the inn when Belinda approached.

Grace laughed. "I wouldn't say that."

"You might say my relationships never get far since a witch that can talk to her cat is pushing the weirdo envelope a little," I said with a laugh.

Grace reached her arm around me and gave me a quick squeeze. "Sometimes I think Wilber's trying to make Belinda jealous."

I scanned the guests. Finding a murderer among this merry bunch felt like an impossible task. "Belinda shared her concerns about you taking over the inn. I'm not sure what to make of her. Why does she spend so much time here when she has her own place in town? It has to be more than because Wilber is welcome."

"She lives alone. I'm sure that gets lonely. The staff here have become like family to her," Grace said.

"It's a pretty expensive family when you have to pay to stay. She must do okay."

Grace shrugged. "Mid was giving her a huge discount. Aunt Mid's big heart was part of the reason she had so much debt. Belinda is probably wondering whether I'll continue to give her a lower rate. I think Aunt Mid did it because she was being kind, plus she didn't have many guests, anyway. Hopefully tonight's event will enable us to book up the rooms again, at least until Christmas."

I latched on to her comment. "You're sure the inn is what you want? Will it make you happy?"

"I think I always knew what my decision would be, but I wasn't ready to admit it. It's not just taking over the inn and the mountain of debt; it's leaving Florida to move back to Pennsylvania." She turned to me. "You're going to have to promise to visit and bring Ava."

"Of course, I'll come. You can't get away from me that easy. And like I could keep Ava away! My sister would've been here in a heartbeat if she didn't have to work." I nodded toward the realtor's sign still leaning against the side of the inn. "Are you putting that out with the trash?"

Grace smiled, taking in the people milling around the front of the inn. "Probably, but more likely, I'll give it back to Janice. It has her picture on it, after all. I doubt she'd want it thrown out with the trash."

"Do you think your change of heart will upset her?" I pulled my sweater tighter over my black dress and tights. My witch costume, complete with the expected pointy hat, was great for the dance but too thin for the cool outside air.

"Maybe, but she'll have to break the news to the interested buyer that Kringle Inn isn't for sale." She lifted the sign and set it behind one of the pine trees decorated with rings of construction paper made by the children at the craft table. "There. Out of sight. Out of mind," she said.

"Wonderful. I think you're making the right decision. You're the perfect woman, and witch, for the job." I stepped forward to stamp down the ground that had pulled loose when she'd moved the sign and then paused. I glanced up. The balcony was above us. The sign had probably been right about where Aunt Mid had fallen. "You would've made your Aunt Mid proud."

"I hope so. She left big shoes to fill." Grace hugged herself against the chill of the wind.

"You mean more like she left big stockings to fill?" My comment drew a smile from Grace. She was wearing the candy cane stockings. "Those are adorable on you."

The wind picked up and blew the sign forward to thump against the tree.

The sign.

I retrieved it from where Grace had set it and looked at Janice's smiling photograph on the corner of the sign. "Janice." I glanced back to the balcony. Had Mid been trying to tell me something else when she was pointing down? Not that she fell from the balcony, but why she fell, and who was responsible by pointing at Janice's picture? "What did Janice tell you about the prospective buyer?"

Grace shrugged. "They wanted to change the place to catch up with the times. She said that people had tired of having Christmas pushed down their throats all year. Heck, if I didn't know better, I'd think you were the buyer."

I barked out a laugh. "You don't have any worries there. I'll stick with being a cocktail waitress. Besides, none of the staff would listen to me. Half the time, even *I* don't follow my own advice."

I paused. "What do you think she meant about catching up with the times? Do you think she meant they wanted to tear the inn down and build something new?" I stepped aside to let a few people pass me and enter the inn.

Grace's expression faltered. "I suppose. I didn't want to know, so I didn't ask. Janice talked about how the holidays are too stressful. Then went on about how the town needs a day spa so people can relax and forget about their troubles—and the holiday. The inn has been in my family...well, since we built it, as far as I know. I didn't want to think about being the one who lost it."

"What about the other implications that might come with the destruction?" I wasn't sure if Grace knew the bigger picture about the responsibilities tied to the inn. I felt her out before she made this commitment. "Couldn't it ruin Christmas for more than just the people of this town? Would it mean the end of Christmas spirit?"

Grace stared up at the inn, which was decorated with twinkling lights. "I don't know. Aunt Mid used to tell me about that when I was a kid. I thought it was a story. A fairy tale. But after staying here, and meeting the people of the town, I believe it, to a degree. But Christmas has changed over the years, as well. Maybe the inn wasn't keeping up by sticking with the old ways. People want things to be shiny and new."

I gestured to the crowds of people. "It sure seems

like people are enjoying these old traditions just fine *without* something shiny and new. They needed to be reminded that change isn't always necessary. Traditions and family are the most important gifts." I glanced at the sign again.

Grace's eyes were wide. "My goodness, I can't believe the inn has finally turned you on to the Christmas spirit. This might be the biggest surprise yet."

"You know me. I'm full of surprises," I said, preparing to lay another revelation on her.

19

I took a deep breath, regretting that I had to puncture this auspicious moment. "Do you think Janice might be the buyer? That she wanted the inn for herself?"

I didn't add—that she might have murdered her aunt.

Grace frowned. "Janice? She doesn't care for the inn. Her disdain is even more obvious than yours. Besides, why wouldn't she say if she was the buyer?"

I shrugged. "I don't know. Perhaps she was trying to get a lower price. Maybe she wanted it for something else." I looked toward the vendor tables. Janice had a multitude of products promising to create a spa in your home. "Like a day spa?"

"A spa? Why? She's a realtor. Sure, she sells those beauty products, but I can't imagine her doing more than that," Grace said. "I don't think she makes much with the products. They aren't very good."

"She could afford it. I heard she came into money when she divorced her husband and moved here." I hadn't heard it, but Jasper had while lingering in the kitchen listening to the staff. Although, he'd also heard that Mid had written Sabina up more than once and that she might've been bitter about that. In retrospect, I'm glad she wasn't holding that against Grace or me, or the eye spy spell she had given me could have had a disastrous outcome.

Grace waved to the people as they went by, acting as the perfect hostess. "Still, if she came into money, buying the inn would be an enormous investment of time, as well."

"Not as much of an investment with a price reduction. Say from multiple deaths?" It was a stretch, but Janice had just become my number one suspect.

Grace paused. "It's all speculation, and you've been spending *way* too much time on this. All you've done is worry and work on the ball. You should go in and enjoy it. Besides, it's not like you could prove it, anyway. And it won't bring Mid back."

"But she could be dangerous," I said, hugging myself against the cool breeze.

"Janice? What is she going to do, perfume me to death?" Grace chuckled and walked away.

I looked up to the balcony again and thought that might've been exactly what Janice had done.

❧

THE UPSTAIRS WAS QUIET. MY ATTEMPT AT STEALTH probably wasn't necessary since the music from the dance echoed throughout the inn. I'd barely been able to get away for a few minutes with the demand for my specialty cocktails. My Christmas wish had come true. My cocktails were a hit for both the magical and mortal, and no one had yet to complain of indigestion or any other adverse effects.

The pieces were all falling into place. Sure, I was relying on my intuition, but I'd played that card before and had come out lucky in gaining the truth. Hopefully, I had some luck left today.

I'd looked everywhere but couldn't find Janice. Maybe she wasn't here.

One more place to check.

We'd closed off the internal, and only external, balconies during the dance. Grace was afraid of risking increases in her insurance after Mid's accident. Combining my specialty cocktails with a balcony was probably not the best idea.

I slowly opened the door to the outside balcony from Mid's, and now Grace's, office. "I thought I might find you here." Janice turned from looking out over the grounds when I approached.

I walked out with Mulder on my heels. "Don't you feel guilty revisiting the scene of the crime?"

"What are you talking about? I came out here for fresh air." She fanned her hand in front of her face. Her flushed skin made her appear overheated, but I thought guilt, or one of her heavily scented lotions or perfumes, was at fault.

"You were listening to me when I was in the library the other day and in the hall earlier tonight. You came to see if what I said was true. You're looking for Mid's spirit." I strode towards her with more confidence than I felt. I had no potion or magic ready to call upon, and Mulder kept bumping against my calves. Doing this the mortal way was riskier and more dangerous than I had expected. But it was the only way to prove her guilt.

"Her spirit? Don't be ridiculous." She glanced around the balcony as if she didn't think the idea was all that absurd and moved away from the edge.

The curtains blew into the ballroom since I'd left the double doors open and created the perfect scene for Jasper to come strolling through. The black cat on Halloween night with a full moon in the sky played perfectly with my plan. Janice watched him approach with trepidation and pulled back when he jumped to the ledge.

I tensed. Jasper had reassured me he had perfect balance, but the thought of him walking on what was equivalent to a ledge not much wider than a tightrope was nerve-wracking. But that was why he did it.

He approached Janice while holding an unwavering stare just to her right. Janice followed his gaze and then looked back to me.

"You've heard about black cats and Halloween, haven't you?" I didn't know what I was implying she'd heard, but I knew many people had irrational thoughts about black cats, especially at Halloween. I intended to play upon those groundless fears.

"He sees Mid," I said.

He didn't.

Mulder wandered back into Grace's office and was staring fixedly at the corner of the room. The sound of snorting and tapping of toenails announced Wilber's entrance into the room. He joined Mulder in starting at the corner. Most likely, *that* was where Mid's spirit lingered.

Janice moved toward the double doors to reenter, and I stepped in front of her. Not enough that she couldn't push me aside if she wanted to get through—which she did—but enough to make her hesitate.

It was time. I followed her into the office, hoping I'd pushed her far enough. I clicked the remote, hoping my memory was correct, and I only changed the music to the microphone and recording system in this room, otherwise it might've alerted Janice if all the music halted.

"Just admit it, Janice. It will help your conscience." I took a step closer. The wind picked up and blew through the open balcony doors to toss my hair about my head.

"Admit what? I have nothing to admit other than irritation at you following me out here. I just wanted quiet. That darn music is so loud." Janice peered around as if still looking for Mid's spirit.

"You mean to the balcony where you last saw Mid before you pushed her to her death? Admit it. Mid didn't commit suicide. She didn't have an accident. You pushed her because you wanted the inn for yourself. She would not sell it to you. Not when you told her you were going to change it into a day spa. No matter how many people you drove away from staying here, Mid wouldn't change her mind."

Janice straightened and met my gaze. "It was an accident." She ran her hand through her hair. "No matter. You can say what you want and think what you like. You're a newcomer, and you don't even like

Christmas. All you've done is stir up trouble since the moment you arrived."

"Wilber? Where are you?" Belinda's voice carried down the hall as she approached the office.

Time was running out; I had to get Janice to confess.

"You're saying you killed Mid?" I felt like a parrot repeating the question but wanted to make sure her full confession was clearly broadcast. "But why? She was a sweet woman whom everyone loved. She brought the magic of Christmas into this town."

Janice made a dismissive sound. "No. For the last time, I didn't kill her. Blah, blah, blah, and the magic of Christmas. No one cares anymore. The town is dying because they hang on to those old traditions. Let it go already. People want to relax and avoid the stress of the holiday season. A day spa would revitalize the town and bring in business. The new owner had agreed that they would feature my products. It would be good for everyone."

"Good for everyone except Mid," I said.

She sighed. "I told you. That was an accident. I would never have hurt Mid. This was a solution to help her get out of debt. I wanted her to try my products to convince her the day spa would be a great idea," she said with a frown. "It's hard to make much money off the products alone. If people could try them at a spa, they might buy them and purchase treatments, like facials or massages." Janice frowned. "It didn't matter. Mid wasn't interested. We went out on the balcony so Mid could see the shimmer of the lotion under the moonlight."

She kept a wary eye on Jasper. "Well, actually she claimed she was allergic to the perfume sample I sprayed and needed some air. She was coughing so I went to get her a glass of water. When I returned, she'd slipped and fell over the edge of the balcony."

Janice wiped a tear away. "I did hear you talking about Mid and seeing spirits," she said and glanced my way. "I almost hoped it was true because I wanted to tell her that I was sorry. She wouldn't have been out on the balcony if it wasn't for my perfume."

A scream and the shattering of glass made us both jump and turn to see Belinda staring fixedly at the corner with Mulder and Wilber.

Then I saw it, too.

Mid's spirit.

And then, she disappeared.

Belinda had dropped her drink glass to shatter and had her hand pressed to her chest. "Is this some kind of trick?" she gasped. "Mid? How is this possible? I'm sorry." She took a step away from Mid's spirit.

Janice furrowed her brow and looked from

Belinda to the corner. She obviously wasn't seeing Mid as the rest of us were. "Belinda? What are you talking about?"

I looked from Janice to Belinda. Could Janice be telling the truth? That she wasn't responsible? Wilber had been there the night Mid died. Wherever Wilber went, Belinda usually wasn't far behind.

"You came into the office after Janice went to get water, didn't you?" I took a step toward Belinda.

Belinda gasped when Mid's spirit briefly shimmered into view and then disappeared again.

"You pushed Mid from the balcony," I said as the pieces fell into place.

"It...it was an accident," Belinda said, her eyes wide and fixed on Mid before her image faded.

"But if it was an accident, why didn't you tell anyone? If it was an accident, you had no reason not to explain what happened." I paused. "That's because it wasn't an accident. You might not have planned it, but when an opportunity presented itself to get Mid out of the picture, you took it. You just weren't planning on Grace."

Belinda's expression hardened. "Who knew there were more of them in the world? I thought she was the last of her bloodline. Mid would never sell. The inn is in this dreadful state because she didn't care for it properly. Then, you two had to come here and try to fix the place up. Getting everyone thinking about the inn again after no one has given a candy cane's worth of bother about this place for years. I could've made it great again. I love the inn—not like the rest of you all who have left it to rot."

"You decreased the value even more by killing Steve?" I knew she didn't kill Steve, but I wanted to see how she would react.

"Who?"

"The man who was working here. They found him dead in the poinsettias."

"Him? I had nothing to do with him. And you say you can—"

I switched the microphone off then. "I can, and I see spirits. How else would I know what happened to Mid?" No need to tell her it was a temporary thing, thanks to Mulder's help.

Many of the guests were of the paranormal variety, or were in costume, so even if I had broadcasted that I was a witch, it didn't worry me. I'd intentionally dressed for the part tonight just in case.

Mulder rushed over and skidded to a stop between Belinda and me. He looked to her left and let out a yip. The temperature in the room dropped rapidly and continued to fall until my breath came out in a cloud of moisture.

Janice backed away from us, hugging herself from

the chill. "What is going on? I'm going to get Grace." She turned and hurried from the room.

I ignored her comment and watched Belinda. It should've been apparent soon enough.

Belinda rubbed her arms and looked at Mulder. "Why is he staring at me?"

I could no longer see Mid, but even I knew what he was looking at. I smiled. "He's not staring at you."

Belinda looked to her left and stumbled back on her heels. "Mid? This isn't a parlor trick?" She twisted her head from side to side as if she might suddenly glimpse her spirit. "Oh, my god; I think she touched me."

Belinda scurried behind the desk, and I stood wondering what I should do. I decided on nothing. Belinda was here, and I'd gotten her confession. I could only hope it had gotten to the right ears. Now it was up to Mid to decide her fate.

"I'm sorry. I ... I really ... I didn't mean for you to fall. You were being so darn stubborn. If only you'd taken the time to consider my offer. You would've agreed that it was for the best." She lurched away, continuously trying to pinpoint where Mid's spirit might've been.

Belinda hadn't realized she was playing a losing game from the start. Mid was a gifted witch who cared for the inn much more than Belinda could ever have dreamed of. “You couldn't let it go, could you?” I said. “You and Wilber already had the run of the place and Mid discounted your rate to stay, but you still wanted more. You wanted it all.”

Anger burned through Belinda’s expression. “You know nothing about me. Think what you want and say what you want. No one will believe you, anyway. I'm leaving.” She turned to exit the room but instead bounced off Nick.

She gasped, but then quickly composed herself. “Oh, Nick. I was just leaving. I came up here to get a little air.”

Nick blocked the doorway. “Belinda Moore, you're under arrest.”

“For what? Is this part of a prank for the Halloween party?” A nervous laugh escaped her lips.

“No, you're under arrest for murdering Mid Loset.” Nick pulled out a pair of handcuffs and held them in front of him. I moved closer behind Belinda in case she gave him any trouble, although I wasn't sure how much help I could’ve been.

“How did you ...” Belinda glanced at me and frowned, perhaps wondering how I'd shared this information so quickly. “I don't know what you're talking about. Surely, you can't believe her. She doesn't even care about Christmas, the inn, or anyone in this town—not like I do.”

"She didn't tell me. You did," Nick said. "You confessed over the loudspeaker. Many thought it was part of the entertainment at first, until you said Mid's name. No one would joke about murdering a beloved member of our community." Nick's expression hardened. "You not only killed Mid; you wanted to kill off Christmas."

Belinda backed up but stopped abruptly when Mulder growled. "But... But... I did nothing; it was an accident."

Nick slapped the cuffs on Belinda. "Save it for the judge. Try swaying him to take you off the naughty list. You're getting a lot worse than coal for Christmas this year."

20

Grace was sealing an envelope to pay off the last of the outstanding bills when I entered the office. "You did it. You saved the inn, and you saved Christmas," she said.

"I wouldn't go that far. We did it—together," I said with a shrug, uncomfortable with the praise.

Grace smiled. "How are you going to deal with Christmas? Are you keeping your new holiday spirit or going back to your bah-humbug ways?"

"I wouldn't say I ever had bah-humbug ways, but I think I've turned some of this town on to Halloween. They might want to keep up the tradition. You can have this combination dance yearly, and then another one before Christmas, if you want to kick it up a notch. But I think I might take a little holiday spirit home with me to Florida. I assume you're going to be moving here?" I knew it was best for Grace, and it was what she wanted, but I hated that my friend wouldn't be so close to me anymore.

Grace nodded. "Yes, but I'm not sure I'll be able to keep the momentum going and ensure the inn prospers. This was one event. A big one for sure, but the Kringle Inn has to keep the Christmas spirit alive all year long."

"Don't worry, you have help here to ensure it succeeds," I said, turning to the mural she'd had painted on her office walls. It depicted the town and all those who cared about the inn, and who would come to care about Grace as I did. That part, I had no doubt. The mural featured Aunt Mid in many of the scenes, as well as a dedicated memorial section for Steve.

Grace smiled. "I do, don't I? Do you know Sabina confessed that she'd hidden some of the outstanding bills from Mid? She knew Mid couldn't pay them, and she couldn't stand seeing Mid so upset or bear the thought of the inn going bankrupt. I think some of the staff might love the inn even more than me. They'll be able to help nurture the holiday spirit, whether or not they're magical."

"Hey. I got you something." I held out a box wrapped in bright Christmas paper with a jolly red bow. "A big change from my usual newspaper wrapping job, huh?"

Grace accepted the gift with a frown. "But it's not Christmas yet. I was hoping you'd come back and spend Christmas here like we talked about."

I shrugged. "I might. I'll have to see what's going on with work and with Gran. Although, I see you hung a stocking for me on the mantle with the rest of the ones for the staff." I was secretly pleased that she'd done so.

"You're just saying that because you want to get as far away from all things Christmas as possible," Grace smiled as she shook the box.

"Actually, I'm not," I said. "You may have finally helped me understand what the Christmas season is all about." I didn't add how this place had given me hope that the magic surrounding it, that I'd dismissed as a child, still existed.

"Does that mean you'll stop calling it consumerism Christmas?" Grace laughed.

"Maybe, but don't get your hopes up," I said.

"Then why did you get me a gift? I got you one, but I expected nothing from you. You've done so much already by helping at the inn and planning the holiday ball. And you made sure Aunt Mid was at peace. I can't thank you enough."

"What are friends for?" I pushed the gift at her,

becoming embarrassed at all her fussing. "Just open it."

She tore the paper with her usual childlike enthusiasm and pulled out the framed photograph. The photo was of Grace smiling broadly, looking very much like her aunt, and just as happy. In the picture, she was looking up at Nick. I'd captured the moment right after Nick and Grace found themselves under the mistletoe I'd strategically placed there for that purpose. Without a little push, they might've taken forever to see what was right in front of them.

"When did you take this?" Her eyes misted over as she studied the picture.

"Right before the dance. Now you can add your frame to the wall with the others. You're part of the history of the Kringle Inn now, and its future." I had a feeling Nick might become a more permanent part of the inn, as well. It helped me feel a little better about her staying behind. She would have someone she could count on—someone who would look out for her.

Grace pulled me into a hug. "It's perfect."

"I know. Who would have imagined I could be thoughtful?" I said.

"I guess I'll give you my gift now, as well." Grace opened her desk drawer and pulled out an elaborately wrapped box, handing it to me.

I gently shook the box. It was a similar size and shape to the one she'd opened, though the wrapping was nicer than mine. I pulled off the wrapping paper and revealed a framed photo.

"Great minds think alike," Grace said, draping her arm around me as we studied the photo together.

The photo depicted me and my little fur-family of Jasper and Mulder. We were decorating the hall. "You had to get me in those candy cane tights and Santa hat, didn't you?"

"Of course. No one would ever believe me about how much I'd gotten you into the Christmas spirit here if I didn't have proof. It needs to go on the wall with the other photos. Everyone might not realize it, but I know if it wasn't for you and your furry detectives, the future for the Kringle Inn might not be nearly as bright."

I wiped the moisture pooling in the corner of my eye. My throat felt thick with emotion. "Thank you."

The lights in the room flickered and then brightened. "Would you look at that." Grace walked over to the window. "It's snowing. I've heard the stories about the inn, and how magic and the Christmas spirit feed off emotions. I think perhaps turning the most bah-humbug witch on to Christmas might've been enough to give us an early snow."

"I can't take credit for that." But it made me

wonder if I was imagining that the mural in the office looked a little brighter than it had a few minutes ago. The lights on the trees seemed to twinkle more brightly.

"How are you doing?" Grace asked. "I haven't taken the time to talk to you about how you've been feeling about Sully."

"Actually, I'm doing pretty good. I haven't even given Sully a thought. Besides, it was good that we broke up. Angels have more important things on their minds."

"Marissa." Grace raised a brow.

"No, seriously. I am fine. I think part of the reason I wanted a relationship was so I wouldn't be alone. But I'm not alone. I have good friends, like you, my Gran and all the crazy seniors at the retirement condo, and my furry family members, as well." I smiled. "I'm content."

I reached down to pet Wilber. He'd been sucking up to Grace—probably concerned he'd lost his free rein at the inn since she'd adopted him. "Sully was probably allergic to animals, anyway."

Grace laughed. "You *are* a magnet for animals lately."

"More like the pied piper. I didn't ask for this." I looked at the photo again. "But I can't say I mind."

"Maybe the spell didn't backfire, after all. Maybe

that's exactly how it was supposed to happen." Grace linked her arm in mine as we watched the light snowfall.

"You're going to have to be more specific." I smiled, teasing her. "Which spell?"

Grace raised a brow. "Your ability to talk to Jasper."

"So, you're saying you believe me?" I poked an elbow into her side in jest.

"Haven't I always believed in you? That's what friends are for. To be there when you're up or down, and to believe you when everyone else might think you've lost your mind," Grace said.

"Well, then. I might need you around more than you think."

❧

THE TRIP BACK TO FLORIDA WASN'T THE SAME without Grace. She stayed to keep the momentum going for the Christmas holiday, to help ensure the Kringle Inn would succeed. I knew she'd be fine. She had the staff and Nick. I promised I'd try to come back for the actual Christmas holiday—if I could convince Gran to make the trip. My home was with Gran now, and we might want to have our own holiday at the retirement condo.

It took a lot of Grace's begging to convince me to consider her offer. It already felt like I was celebrating Christmas twice in one year. Once had seemed like more than enough most years, but maybe not anymore. I tried to use the excuse of having to convince my boss, Vlad, to let me off work again, but that excuse fell flat. Grace knew how to manipulate the hearts of many, including ones who didn't really have a beating heart, like Vlad.

The headlights cut through the darkness as the sun rose. Almost home.

I couldn't wait to see Gran and tell her all about the trip. She'd believe every unbelievable word of it. That was one glorious thing about my Gran. But I'd have to swear her to secrecy. If she spoke one word about the secrets of the Kringle Inn, and Mulder seeing ghosts, it would end up in the Willow Words. Then the whole retirement condo would know about it.

I started from my thoughts at the sound of loud snoring coming from the back seat. Maybe the time spent together on the trip, and the magic of the Kringle Inn, would give me another gift. The gift of my favorite fur family members, Mulder and Jasper, finally loving each other—well, starting to.

I glanced in the rearview mirror at the back seat. Mulder and Jasper were both fast asleep and snuggled up against each other. My heart warmed at the sight. If only they could've been this sweet to each other when they were awake.

Well, I never got everything on my Christmas list, but usually, I got all I needed. If I got everything I'd wanted today, that wouldn't be any fun. That would leave nothing to dream about and wish for tomorrow.

Once again, I wondered if my seeing Mid's spirit was a fluke. Did I see her briefly because it was Halloween? Or was this one of the aftereffects Ambrosia had mentioned could result from doing spells messing with spirits? Guess I'd find out if more spirits started showing up. As if I didn't have enough trouble concealing my ability to talk to a cat, let alone spirits.

Who knew what to expect next when it came to magic? That's what makes it so fun.

In case you missed it, read the story that started the adventures of Marissa, Jasper, and Mulder.

My magic might not be up to par, but I'm no killer. The question is, who is?

Curses, Cats & Corpses

A Charmed Cocktail Cozy Mystery

Want more Paranormal Cozy Mystery?

The Witch Shifter Series

These cozy paranormal mysteries feature a shifty witch, a cranky cat, and a whole lot of shenanigans.

WILL YOU HELP OTHER READERS FIND THIS BOOK?

If you have enjoyed this story, it would be wonderful if you would leave a review. Reviews help my books get noticed and bring them to the attention of other readers who may enjoy them.

To leave a review, click below.

Magic Mimosas & Mistletoe

Thank you!

ALSO BY M.L. BONATCH & MAUREEN BONATCH

Welcome to small-town stories with hocus pocus and all that. Enjoy paranormal cozy mystery, and romance by M.L. Bonatch and urban fantasy stories by Maureen Bonatch.

The Charmed Cocktail Cozy Series

Join Marissa Hale in the Charmed Cocktail Cozy series, these cozy paranormal mysteries feature a willful witch, a chatty cat, a delightful dog, and a mystery to solve.

The Witch Shifter Series

These cozy paranormal mysteries feature a shifty witch, a cranky cat, and a whole lot of shenanigans.

The Violet Storm Urban Fantasy Series

Half the time, we're writing the history of these Unknown

paranormal species. That's what I do. I don't have a reference book. I am the reference book.

The Enchantlings Series

This Urban Fantasy story features Hope, as she struggles to determine if her ability to infuse euphoria or despair with her touch makes her the devil's spawn or his exterminator.

Other Standalone Stories

Evil Speaks Softly

They were never supposed to meet.

Fame came easily for Liv by following in the footsteps of the female writers in her family. The cycle repeated for decades...until Liv changed the story. Her villain doesn't like the revision—and he isn't a fictional character. In his story, the bad guy always wins.

Till Death

To protect an innocent man, a dutiful wife challenges her

vengeful husband...with disastrous results.

Follow me on Amazon and sign up for my newsletter so you're one of the first to know when new stories are available.

GET YOUR FREE STORIES

Get several free short stories, including *Spells, Spirits & Stiffs*, exclusive behind-the-scenes excerpts, and be the first to hear about sales and new books. when you sign up for my newsletter.

It's free to sign up, and you can opt out anytime.

Click, or copy and paste this link to sign up and get more magical stories: https://www.maureenbonatch.com/free-book/

Spells, Spirits & Stiffs, A Charmed Cocktail Cozy Mystery

What's worse than a bunch of elderly witches in provocative Halloween costumes? One dead one.

Do you love books, pets, and magic? Then come join my exclusive group- Must Love Magic:

https://www.facebook.com/groups/630494098126926

ABOUT THE AUTHOR

Just a small-town girl, M.L. Bonatch leads a double life. She lives in a magical world, writing cozy paranormal mysteries and sweet, humorous paranormal romance as M.L. Bonatch and urban fantasy as Maureen Bonatch.

While she's not busy writing or doing nurse things, she's a mom to her twin daughters, bicycling in the beautiful woods of PA with her hubby, doing the bidding of a feisty Shih Tzu, and dancing as much as possible. She believes music can be paired with every mood, laughter is contagious, and that caffeine and wine are essential for survival.

Be the first to find out about book sales, new releases, and other fun stuff from her furry sidekick, Scruff, by signing up for her newsletter: https://www.maureenbonatch.com/free-book/

Find all Maureen's stories here: https://www.maureenbonatch.com/

amazon.com/-/e/B0951C41XM
bookbub.com/authors/m-l-bonatch
facebook.com/MLBonatch
instagram.com/mlbonatch.author
twitter.com/mbonatch
pinterest.com/maureenbonatch

www.ingramcontent.com/pod-product-compliance
Lightning Source LLC
La Vergne TN
LVHW090558110826
845146LV00001B/180

* 9 7 9 8 9 8 5 3 5 1 0 3 3 *